Murder in Suffolk

A Chief Inspector Pointer Mystery

By A. E. Fielding

Originally published in 1935

Murder in Suffolk

© 2016 Resurrected Press
www.ResurrectedPress.com

Published by Resurrected Press

This classic book was handcrafted by Resurrected Press. Resurrected Press is dedicated to bringing high quality classic books back to the readers who enjoy them. These are not scanned versions of the originals. but, rather, quality checked and edited books meant to be enjoyed!

Please visit ResurrectedPress.com to view our entire catalogue!

For news and updates, visit us on Facebook! Facebook.com/ResurrectedPress

ISBN 13: 978-1-943403-18-9

Printed in the United States of America

Other Resurrected Press books in *The Chief Inspector Pointer Mystery* Series

RESURRECTED PRESS CLASSIC MYSTERY CATALOGUE

The Uttermost Farthing: A Savant's Vendetta

Arthur Griffiths
The Passenger From Calais
The Rome Express

Fergus Hume
The Mystery of a Hansom Cab
The Green Mummy
The Silent House
The Secret Passage

Edgar Jepson
The Loudwater Mystery

A. E. W. Mason
At the Villa Rose

A. A. Milne
The Red House Mystery

Baroness Emma Orczy
The Old Man in the Corner

Edgar Allan Poe
The Detective Stories of Edgar Allan Poe

Arthur J. Rees
The Hampstead Mystery
The Shrieking Pit
The Hand In The Dark
The Moon Rock
The Mystery of the Downs

Mary Roberts Rinehart
Sight Unseen and The Confession

Dorothy L. Sayers

Whose Body?

Sir William Magnay
The Hunt Ball Mystery

Mabel and Paul Thorne
The Sheridan Road Mystery

Louis Tracy
The Strange Case of Mortimer Fenley
The Albert Gate Mystery
The Bartlett Mystery
The Postmaster's Daughter
The House of Peril
The Sandling Case: What Would You Have Done?

Charles Edmonds Walk
The Paternoster Ruby

John R. Watson
The Mystery of the Downs
The Hampstead Mystery

Edgar Wallace
The Daffodil Mystery
The Crimson Circle

Carolyn Wells
Vicky Van
The Man Who Fell Through the Earth
In the Onyx Lobby
Raspberry Jam
The Clue
The Room with the Tassels
The Vanishing of Betty Varian
The Mystery Girl
The White Alley
The Curved Blades

Anybody but Anne
The Bride of a Moment
Faulkner's Folly
The Diamond Pin
The Gold Bag
The Mystery of the Sycamore
The Come Back

Raoul Whitfield
Death in a Bowl

And much more!
Visit ResurrectedPress.com
for our complete catalogue

FOREWORD

". . . and now for something completely different."
                                        Monty Python

When *Murder in Suffolk* was published, A. E. Fielding had already written twenty-two mysteries featuring Chief-Inspector Pointer as the central character. These were typical examples of the mystery genre in what is often referred to as "The Golden Age of British Mysteries." They featured involved plots, misleading clues, and the complex domestic relations that were so popular in the detective fiction of the time. *Murder in Suffolk* has none of these.

Instead of a mystery, *Murder in Suffolk* is much more of a political thriller. It involves political intrigue, plenty of action, and the sort of conspiracy for which Ian Fleming was to become so famous. It also introduces a new character in the form of private investigator Hugh Duncan, a former Scotland Yard man who, being of independent means, has resigned in favor of a life roaming the world in search of adventure. Pointer is reduced to a minor role, asking Duncan to look into the disappearance of a Scotland Yard detective who has gone missing while on duty in a remote part of Suffolk.

It is interesting to speculate as to the reasons why Fielding should write a novel so unlike her previous books. Was it an attempt to broaden her audience or was she trying to cash in on the public's growing unease on the eve of the Second World War? Had she perhaps become bored with Pointer and the mystery format? Unless new information comes to light, it is unlikely that the answers to these questions will ever be known. What is obvious from reading the book is that Fielding was attempting to launch a new series, and that *Murder in Suffolk* was intended as both an introduction and a transition to this new series.

It is also interesting to speculate as to why these plans for this new series never came to fruition. *Murder in Suffolk* was to be the last book Fielding wrote, either for Pointer or Duncan. One additional book, *Pointer to a Crime* was published some six years later in 1944, but there is some reason to believe that parts of it were ghost written and may have been based on an earlier, unpublished work of Fielding's. It may be that the war or ill-health intervened, but, as so little is known about the author it is impossible say why 1938, for all intents and purposes, marked the end of Fielding's career.

As stated earlier, *Murder in Suffolk* is much more of a thriller than a mystery. It begins with the missing Scotland Yard man and the discovery of a corpse—not the missing man—but it soon becomes clear who the villain is with the only real mystery being what exactly he is up to. There is plenty of action in the form of shootings, gassings, chase scenes and all the other trappings of the genre but not much in the way of detecting. Geopolitics in the form of rival arab states is also part of the story line. Fielding was no stranger to foreign intrigue, and international politics had played a role in several of her earlier works, notable *The Charteris Mystery* (Italian Fascists), *The Clifford Affair*(Basque separatists), and *The Paper-Chase* (German Fascists), but in all those books politics was subsidiary to the real mystery. In *Murder in Suffolk*, politics is at the heart of the matter, perhaps in keeping with the intentions for the new series.

While *Murder in Suffolk* may not be a mystery in the strictest sense of the word, it is a fast paced adventure with plenty of action. It is with great pleasure that Resurrected Press offers its readers this new edition of *Murder in Suffolk*.

About the Author

The identity of the author is as much a mystery as the plots of the novels. Two dozen novels were published from 1924 to 1944 as by Archibald Fielding, A. E. Fielding, or Archibald E. Fielding, yet the only clue as to the real author is a comment by the American publishers, H.C. Kinsey Co. that A. E. Fielding was in reality a "middle-aged English woman by the name of Dorothy Feilding whose peacetime address is Sheffield Terrace, Kensington, London, and who enjoys gardening." Research on the part of John Herrington has uncovered a person by that name living at 2 Sheffield Terrace from 1932-1936. She appears to have moved to Islington in 1937 after which she disappears. To complicate things, some have attributed the authorship to Lady Dorothy Mary Evelyn Moore nee Feilding (1889-1935), however, a grandson of Lady Dorothy denied any family knowledge of such authorship. The archivist at Collins, the British publisher, reports that any records of A. Fielding were presumably lost during WWII. Birthdates have been given variously as 1884, 1889, and 1900. Unless new information comes to light, it would appear that the real authorship must remain a mystery.

Greg Fowlkes
Editor-In-Chief
Resurrected Press
www.ResurrectedPress.com
www.Facebook.com/ResurrectedPress

CHAPTER ONE

The lone hiker seemed to have the world to himself. Behind him the little town of Benham, which he had left an hour before, was now out of sight behind the friendly bulk of the last trees to be seen for some time.

To the right, half a mile distant, but drawing closer with each stride he took, was the North Sea. Away to the left was the rolling heath country that marched into the west.

Ahead of him was a lonely, sandy waste of country, known as Little Sahara to the people of that part of Suffolk and the hiker knew that for the whole sixteen miles which he must cover across it, only one thing would break the naked line of sand and sea. That was a gaunt and deserted Martello Tower, which he had been told marked the half-way distance.

But this lonely prospect did not seem to dismay the man. He sniffed the strong air appreciatively as, before leaving the last bit of green turf for the rough track that would be his way, he paused to fill his pipe.

Outlined against the sky, he made a strange figure for that remote spot. He was dressed in khaki shirt and shorts, golf stockings and heavy boots, and to top the outfit, as if in gay salute to the wild places he was traversing, he wore a brilliant green beret. On his back was the inevitable ruck-sack and in one hand he carried a staff or walker's thumbstick.

He started on again, his mind busy with his own thoughts, his eye registering each change in the general prospect. It was without the slightest foreboding that he went plodding across that barren land which had been so aptly named Little Sahara. There was no clairvoyant quality about it to whisper that the Martello Tower, whose only significance to him was, so he thought, that it marked the course, would be the last thing that he would ever see.

Owing to the rolling nature of the sand, piled into dunes and little valleys by the savage winter winds that drive in from the North Sea, he did not catch the first glimpse of the tower until he had covered several miles.

He spied it then as a low, round stump, squatting close to the horizon, and, as he viewed it, seeming to rise right out of the sea. But as he advanced, it rose slowly out of its bed until he could see almost the whole round unlovely structure that had been reared back in the time when Napoleon swore to invade England—and learned that vows do not conquer a nation.

He paused again and knocked his pipe against his heel. Then he took a slow, deliberate view of his surroundings.

The sun was hot on his back, even though it was autumn. Only the lightest of breezes drifted in from the sea. It was more like a day that summer had forgotten.

Yet in the midst of all this quiet and brightness there swept over him a feeling of such sharp depression that the physical revulsion forced him into speech.

"What the devil's the matter with me?" he apostrophised a wheeling gull. "Here it is, the finest day I've seen this year, and not a thing but me and all outdoors, and yet, hang it, I feel as if some one was standing behind me with a bludgeon."

He actually turned to peer about. A gull swooped nearer, screamed in derision, and soared out over the sea. The man recovered his good spirits and laughed.

"I'll be seeing pictures next," he told himself.

"What I need is a spot of food and a swig out of the flask. It's not more than a mile to the old tower, and it'll be nice and shady inside. Forward, my jolly old hiker."

With that, he made to start on again, but as he did so his eye caught something that made him pause.

"Now what was that?" he muttered.

Low down against the sand something had moved. To the man who stood gazing across the sand, it had seemed at first like a bird vanishing into one of the myriad hollows.

Then reason told him it could not be a gull, for the object had appeared black, and no other sort of bird was visible. He hadn't seen a crow in miles.

Another movement caught his eye, this time a little distance from where he had seen the other. He was able now to take more note of its size and form, and to his puzzlement found it could be likened to nothing more than a human head adorned by a cap.

But if this were so then the head must be attached to a body, and the same line of deduction indicated that some one must be crawling along between the dunes.

It was a conclusion that seethed ridiculous. Why should any one choose to move in such surreptitious fashion in this deserted spot? It wasn't as though it were the hour and place for wildfowl. There wasn't one to be found within miles. In the first hours of dawn, farther on, where the muddy creeks cut into the coast, it would be different; but not here.

He saw the movement again, and he knew that, strange though it might seem, the moving speck was indeed a man, and that for some reason or other he was trying to conceal his progress across the sand.

He suddenly realised how plainly visible he himself must be. Indeed, his solitary figure must stand out against that denuded background almost as clearly as the Martello Tower.

Ordinarily he would have trudged on quite openly, but there was something so furtive about the actions of the other man that he was curious to know the reason. He could not be sure, but it seemed to him that the fellow's course was gradually converging on the Martello Tower.

A deep hollow between two dunes gave him the chance he sought. He sank down, eased his ruck-sack from his shoulder and peered over the top.

Minutes passed. Not a thing moved. An Arab of the real Sahara could not have vanished more completely than the figure he had seen. The only thing that reached him was an increased heaviness of spirit which he found impossible to understand or to shake off.

At the end of a quarter of an hour he rose, and giving his broad shoulders a shake as if to rid himself of the invisible load of despondency, slung the ruck-sack into place and strode on purposefully. If there was anything there he would find it on closer approach.

But nearer and nearer though he drew to the tower, not a moving object could be seen except the gulls that wheeled and dipped overhead, berating him, it seemed, for this invasion of their solitude.

He changed his course a little so as to bring him round towards the low entrance, from which he could now see a dilapidated door hanging. He approached it in a direct line, and, when he was a matter of some thirty or forty yards away, could see right into the gloom of the interior. But no detail was visible; only a well of heavy twilight.

Then suddenly he paused. Something emerged from the gloom and appeared in the frame of the doorway. At least, it seemed to the hiker that a human form hovered there for a brief moment before becoming part of the heavy curtain behind.

In any ordinary habitation or building there would have been no sinister suggestion about that fleeting vision. But here, in the broad daylight of this sunny day, in this expanse of utter loneliness, there was something deeply disturbing to the solitary watcher in this furtive movement.

Was it the man whom he had seen before? Or had there been more than one individual creeping through the hollows? Had they reached the tower? Why this surreptitious stalking of some one or something? Was he the quarry? Or was it another whom he hadn't yet discovered?

Whatever the purpose, the watcher saw nothing else as he drew still nearer. He told himself that the prowler he had discovered was no more than some vagrant who had viewed his approach with natural suspicion. He broke into a whistle as he began to feel for the straps of his rucksack. He was thinking that he had been a bit of an old woman to imagine some trick of light and shadow to possess a sinister meaning.

He was close to the door now, and suddenly he saw something move against the twilight. He hesitated on the threshold. The warning in his subconsciousness was so urgent that it was like an invisible hand pressing him back.

He peered into the gloom, but nothing moved. Then he gave voice. "Halo, inside!"

The echoes came back to him muffled; not another sound. He frowned and started forward again. One foot went over the sill, but he never completed the crossing of that threshold alive.

Out of the gloom on either side of the door shadows came upon him, and something descended heavily upon his skull.

CHAPTER TWO

It was at the personal request of Chief-Inspector Pointer of Scotland Yard that Hugh Duncan travelled down into Suffolk. Duncan was a varsity man who had entered the Yard but who had disliked the very strict frame within which he had to work. He had left the Force after a year and set up as a private investigator, with the son of an old servant as his helper. Duncan was well off, and well connected, and was often able to help his former colleagues in some matter which lay outside and yet was connected with criminal cases.

"One of our plain-clothes men, Sergeant Peel, is down there somewhere," Pointer told Duncan. "He is on special duty, which is to keep tabs on the son of an Arab sheik who is visiting this country. This sheik is in the good books of the Foreign Office, and they made a special request that we keep a fatherly eye on him. He's over here for some sort of medical treatment. Arrived with his own medical attendant!"

"Can you give me the father's name?"

"Wait a moment."

Pointer fumbled amongst some papers, and drew out a slip.

"Sheik El Bakr."

"Ah! He is the sheik of El Wejh—a very useful man. Well, why do you want me to go down?"

"To see what Peel is up to. He is supposed to send in a daily report. We haven't had anything for three days."

"Can't you ask the local people to make inquiries?

"No. In the first place we don't want them to know that he is down there. It isn't anything to do with them, but you know what they are. And secondly, the F.O. has made it a point that we are to carry out the job as quietly as possible. For some reason or other they seem to consider this business of great political importance."

"What is the sheik's son doing in Suffolk?"

"In Peel's last report he said he had entered the sanatorium of some doctor down there. I'll have the name here. Yes. Grunevald—Dr. Grunevald."

Duncan nodded.

"I know the name. Dr. Grunevald is a man of high standing in his profession. He specialises, I believe, in nervous ailments."

"That's probably why this young Arab has gone there. But it's Peel I'm worrying about. I can't understand why we haven't heard from him for three days."

"I know Peel," said Duncan. "He always seemed a dependable man."

"One of the best we've got. It isn't that he has gone off on the loose. But he's a little prone to carry things on his own responsibility, and from one or two hints he dropped in his last report, I'm inclined to think he may be following some interesting sideline as well. I haven't the ghost of a notion what it may be. In any event, his job is to keep an eye on his charge. If I send one of our own men down, the local police will be on their dignity. You can handle the matter more diplomatically without arousing suspicion. Will you go, ostensibly on a holiday, but also as a friend of Peel's who wants to have a chat with him, since he too is in the neighbourhood?"

"I don't mind. I expect it will be a mare's nest, but as long as you are paying expenses it won't make any difference to me—nor to Peter. I'll have him follow after me and meet me down there. Just where would I look for the elusive Peel?"

"The last report we had was from a place called Benham. Know it?"

"Very well."

"I'd give you the dossier now, but it's with Superintendent Browne, and he's out. I can send it down in tonight's post."

"That will do."

The upshot was that, after some further discussion, Duncan left London in his car, and late the same afternoon was driving along the single main street of Benham, on the Suffolk coast. He hesitated whether to seek the hotel first or to go at once to the police station. It was the sight of the latter half-way along the street that decided him. He drew up and went in. When he had made himself known he was glad of his decision, for not only was the inspector in charge a cheery soul, but he seemed only too delighted to do anything in his power to accommodate the famous detective. Indeed, before their interview was over, Inspector Clark had made Duncan promise that he would not go to the inn, but would use Clark's cottage as his headquarters during his stay in Benham.

But regarding Peel of the Yard he could be of little assistance.

"I don't know him. He certainly didn't call on us, Mr. Duncan. If you will give me a description of him, I shall have inquiries made and let you know where he's staying. But I think he must have left Benham."

Duncan gave him the necessary details. Inspector Clark despatched his own sergeant to the hotel to start inquiries, and while they waited he took Duncan to his own cottage for a cup of tea.

It was not until after the evening meal, however, that Duncan was in possession of all that Sergeant Reford could learn, which, indeed, was very little.

He could find no one who seemed to have noticed any one answering to the details of the description given him. Duncan had said that Peel had probably left Benham on foot. This had been told him by Chief Inspector Pointer, who had it from Peel's last report, in which Peel had said that he intended walking from Benham to Little Soham, some sixteen miles farther up the coast.

It seemed that Benham was not invaded by many, tourists, neither by the sort that is known as "hikers" nor by the more common variety of tramp.

Sergeant Reford had particulars of a few strangers who had passed through the town, and of one who was undoubtedly a "hiker," as his garb had been easily distinguishable, the most conspicuous item being a bright green beret. But there was nothing among the few items that seemed to relate to Peel. It was certainly not easy to picture that staid and sober officer flaunting such a piece of headgear.

One thing, however, was definite. Any one going on foot from Benham to Little Soham would almost certainly go by the track that led more or less parallel with the coast, and in doing so crossed a barren, sandy waste of land known locally as Little Sahara. To go by any other route would mean a journey some eight or ten miles longer, by way of the road that curved across the heath.

On weighing up the little information he had to go on, Duncan was inclined to think that the shorter road would be the one Peel would follow, for by discreet inquiries he managed to elicit the fact that the sanatorium run by Dr. Grunevald could be reached that way, and it seemed that the charge in whom Peel was interested was now a resident patient in that place.

He made his arrangements, therefore, to start off the next day and follow what he thought would be the path taken by Peel. Inspector Clark had telephoned to Little Soham and made inquiries there, but without any encouraging result.

Clark offered, too, to drive Duncan across Little Sahara in his own two-seater, a car that he affirmed would handle the rough road better than a horse. But Duncan declined with thanks. He intended to go the way that Peel would probably have chosen—supposing him to have made for the sanatorium.

He left Benham at mid-morning, dressed in rough tweeds, strong boots, a cap, and carrying a stout cudgel that Clark had lent him.

A quarter of an hour saw him out of Benham, with the town, or rather village, out of sight behind the trees. Then, on topping a rise, he saw the desolate waste of Little Sahara before him, and finding the rough track, set off at a brisk stride, his pipe sending out a cloud of fragrant smoke as he went.

The rough track changed to hard-pack, swept clean by the strong gales that blow from the North Sea. It wound gradually nearer and nearer to the sea until, when Duncan caught his first glimpse of the stump that was the Martello Tower, there was only a narrow strip of dunes between him and the beach.

Far out at sea he could just discern the sails of a couple of fishing boats, and still farther, a smudge of smoke that he guessed came from a coasting steamer, or perhaps from some ship out of the Thames making for a Scandanavian port. For the rest, he was alone with the gulls that screamed in dreary chorus as they followed his course.

He held to the path until he had almost reached the tower. Then, just as he was about to turn up the short path to go in at the door, he paused and gazed intently at the sand in front of him.

After a moment he dropped to his knees to examine more closely the marks that had caught his eye. But he soon rose again, for he found that at such close quarters the loose, sand made them confusing. By backing away a little and changing his position so that the sun came from one side, he found that he could distinguish them more clearly.

They seemed to be parallel lines that could be followed for a short distance in the sand before they vanished in the hard-pack. When he walked along the main track he found that again and again he could distinguish the same traces. Then he came to a wider part of the road, where the ground was windswept so clean that the marks disappeared entirely.

At one place, where they showed more clearly than at any other, he dropped to his knees again, and with the aid of his cudgel made a rough measurement. It served to strengthen his theory that the marks had been left by the passage of some sort of vehicle, either a wheeled cart or even a sledge. He was puzzled to imagine what the vehicle could have been doing at such a spot as this.

It was quite possible that some one might have driven a cart across Little Sahara from, say, Benham to Little Soham. But, he argued to himself, if that were so, then why hadn't he noticed similar tracks before he reached the tower; for he was perfectly certain that he would have done so had there been any to see.

He retraced his, steps and, pausing on the threshold, gazed into the gloom of the interior. It was very still and quiet. Even the gulls seemed to have stopped screaming.

He saw a rickety table and a couple of packing-cases, some drifted sand, scraps of paper, burnt matches, cigarette-ends, and a few empty tins. It was plain that the place had been used as a halt or doss-house by tramps and other vagrants, who had not troubled to clear up the litter they had caused.

He stepped inside and made a tour of the circular walls. Nothing of interest rewarded him. He was debating whether to pull up one of the packing-cases as a seat and have his lunch now, or to push on to Little Soham, when his eye fell on a tumbledown staircase that led to the floor above.

It looked far too precarious to bear the weight of a man, and many of the steps were missing entirely, but Duncan decided to test it.

He ascended gingerly, the rotten wood creaking and swaying in an alarming way. It held together, however, and reaching the top, he stepped cautiously into the room above.

It occupied the whole diameter of the tower and was about the same height as the room beneath except for the added space of the vaulted roof area.

There was no furniture, and it was half-filled with sand which apparently had drifted in through the two windows, which had neither panes nor shutters. A ladder went up towards the roof, from the top of which it looked as though one could get out on to the gallery which Duncan had already noticed ran round the outside of the tower.

He determined to finish the job of exploration. Reaching the top of the ladder, he crawled out on to the platform. He tested the boards carefully. They sagged beneath him, but held. He stood up and ventured as far as the remains of what had once been a guard-rail.

Now he could see across Little Sahara for a considerable distance. Away to his right were the roofs of Little Soham, for which he was bound. Close to the village were shadowy patches of purple and green, where the marsh flats ran into the saltings.

Straight ahead the sandy wastes turned to the bright green of heath, which was backed by lines of wind-driven pine. It was in this direction that he caught sight of the roof of what he took to be a large house. It seemed to be about two miles distant. He wondered if this could be the sanatorium run by Dr. Grunevald. The place ought to be about there. He saw not a sign of a human being. Apparently he had the whole of Little Sahara to himself.

He made his way back down the ladder, but did not continue at once to the lower room. While viewing the heap of sand from above, it struck him that it was an extraordinarily large quantity to have drifted in through the windows, even though the fierce gales from the North Sea, particularly in winter, must fill the air with the loose fabric of Little Sahara.

He crunched his way across to where the heap began to pile against the wall. He began to toe away the sand with his foot, sweeping it from side to side.

Then suddenly, close into the stone wall, his boot struck something hard. He bent quickly, and scraped away with his hands. Now he uncovered an object which had not come there by the force of any wind, no matter how mighty the gale. He dashed away more and more of the sand until he could catch hold of the object and drag it out.

It yielded less readily than he expected. It was very heavy. He exerted still more strength. It moved, and then, as the holding sand fell away, came towards him with such speed that it fetched up against his foot painfully.

He could see now that it was a small cask, and he could hear the sound of some liquid sloshing about inside.

The next half-hour was fully occupied by Duncan in a further delving into the heap of sand. His efforts were by no means barren. On the contrary, they were rewarded by the discovery of six more casks exactly similar to the first, and a much smaller object that intrigued him far more than the casks.

This was a small black leather note-book that he came upon beneath one of the casks. It contained several pages of pencilled notes. Reading them carefully, although only initials and other abbreviations were used he was able to fill in the blanks sufficiently to reach the startling conclusion that what he had found was nothing more nor less than Detective-Sergeant Peel's private note-book.

How had it come to be in such a place? How had it found its way beneath a cask of what he knew to be contraband brandy, a cask hidden in this old Martello Tower on Little Sahara?

He studied the note-book again.

Most of the few pages which bore any writing dealt with the movements of the young Arab whom Peel had been told off to watch.

The notes began in London, and bore plain reference to the young man and to the Hotel Venetia, where he had stayed. Later there was a full sentence which stated that

Peel had travelled down from London and had seen his charge enter the private sanatorium run by Dr. Grunevald.

Following this were other abbreviated references which seemed to indicate that Peel was following routine duties, and that his charge was still in the same place. In among these were some separate entries which puzzled Duncan exceedingly. They were disjointed, very cryptic, and apparently bore little connection one with the other. If, however, Peel had had reason to write cryptically, then he might deliberately have made the entries as confusing as possible.

They had been jotted down on three different pages, and, as Duncan saw them, appeared as follows:

First page.—A. F. . . . L. S. . . . 19-18 n.g.

Second page.—A. F. . . . p.b. . . . 40 knots.

Third page.—Fr. Cr. . . . camouf (?) . . . Thurs. (?). . . . A.F.

Not very enlightening at a first perusal, but Duncan knew from experience that a little analysis and reconstruction would sometimes put meaning into the most obscure writing. He dropped the little book into his pocket to tackle again later.

At the moment the question to be solved was how the book had found its way beneath the cask of contraband brandy in this heap of sand.

He remembered what Pointer had said about Peel's report suggesting that the latter had run into something interesting down in Suffolk. Was it this contraband?

Duncan knew quite a lot about the smuggling that takes place along that stretch of coast, which, with its secluded little creeks, is an ideal spot for the purpose. And to sniff the bungs of these tasks before him, as well as to read the name "Rotterdam" cut in the wood at each end, was all he had needed to tell him that he had stumbled on a nice little packet of smuggled brandy. Peel was hardly likely to have been duller-witted. Had he, for instance, seen something that suggested smuggling while he was prowling about Little Sahara, keeping an eye on his charge? And as a consequence had he, when the coast was clear, searched the tower until he had discovered the cache beneath the sand, and dropped his note-book while doing this?

It seemed a reasonable enough theory, to be sure, but what of the question that the chief-inspector at the Yard wanted answered? What had become of Peel?

Duncan resumed his search until he had turned over all the sand in the heap. Nothing more rewarded his search. He left the casks as they were and descended the stairs to the ground-floor room.

When he had finished a hasty lunch, he did not, as he had intended, continue his way to Little Soham. He got out the note-book again, and after reading the entries through from beginning to end he set himself to study the cryptic items.

It was after four o'clock when he rose and prepared to walk back to Benham. He had decided that it was better to approach Little Soham from another angle, for certain things in Peel's puzzling items caused him to wonder more and more upon what the Yard man could have stumbled.

Furthermore, he must at once inform Inspector Clark of the cache in the tower. That settled, Duncan put the note-book away, and filling his pipe afresh, stepped into the open.

The traces of what he had taken to be cart or sledge-tracks caught his attention afresh. He could make a better guess now as to their meaning. That contraband brandy would have needed some sort of vehicle for its transport. He traced them carefully, inch by inch, now losing them, now finding them again, trying to discover if they took any definite direction.

Suddenly he saw an object in the sand, a little to one side of the tracks and against the sloping bank of one of the dunes. From any other place but where he knelt it would have been invisible.

He walked towards it, and as he got close, saw that it was the sole of a boot, the upturned sole, and it did not take much deduction to guess that it had been uncovered by some chance shifting of the sand.

It was a very smart-looking sole—hand-welted. He began to scrape away the surrounding grit. Then, as he saw what was gradually coming to light, his digging became savagely urgent.

The body of a man became revealed, it lay face upwards, with the mouth, nostrils and ears choked with sand. And one glance was enough to tell Duncan that the man was no Nordic, for his skin was the brown of sepia and his hair the oily black of the East.

He was clad in a suit of cheap black serge; his feet were encased in black patent shoes with very pointed toes. A broad-brimmed black hat lay crumpled beneath one shoulder. The man's skull had been smashed in with terrific force, and pressed into the sand by the weight of the body was an implement that looked a likely weapon. It was the broken tiller-handle of a boat.

Duncan freed it gently from the sand, and lifting it, scrutinised it closely. On the heavier end were stains that he felt sure were blood, for adhering to them were several hairs that matched those on the dead man's head.

Duncan spent several minutes examining this crude weapon, then, before replacing it where he had found it, he took a pair of tweezers from his pocket and drew a few hairs from where they clung. These he placed carefully in an envelope for further examination.

It was odd that he should make such a gruesome discovery while seeking a clue to the whereabouts of Sergeant Peel. He wondered if there could be any connection between this corpse and the secret cache of brandy that he had found. If Peel was lying very low, and digging into some sinister business down here, Duncan certainly didn't want to take any steps that would spoil his game. On the other hand, here was something that must be reported to the local police, and it was his duty to carry that report.

He began to scrape the loose sand over the body. He was thinking that the broken tiller-handle that had been used as a weapon was a direct link with some seafaring person or persons, but that did not mean that such a person had used it for murder. If it had been discarded it could have been picked up by any, one. Nevertheless the thought was enough to cause Duncan again to turn a speculative eye in the direction of Little Soham.

He was more glad than ever that he had decided to approach the place in a different way. When he had finished, he rose, and started off at a long stride towards Benham. He hated leaving the poor remains alone, but there was no other way. As he strode along, so absorbed was be in his own thoughts that he did not see the form of a man slither along the sand between two of the dunes and cautiously lift his head to watch him until he was out of sight. Nor did he know that the same pair of eyes had been spying on his movements for the past hour or more.

Back in Benham he made his report to the local inspector, to whom he did not disclose the fact that he had also found a note-book, a note-book that he thought belonged to Sergeant Peel.

The inspector lost no time in leaving for the tower in his two-seater car, insisting that Duncan should make himself comfortable at the cottage until his return. Following the car went a man from a local garage with his van.

When he had seen them off, Duncan walked to the post office and sent a telegram to his assistant Peter, instructing him to come down to Benham that evening. Then he strolled along to Clark's cottage.

He was still sitting before the fire, smoking, when Clark came in. The moment he saw the other's face, Duncan knew that a hitch had occurred somewhere.

"We found the body all right, Mr. Duncan, and Tom Hatt has brought it in his van. But those casks of brandy you said we'd find in the upper room of the tower, there wasn't a sign of anything of the sort. There's nothing but sand in the place."

CHAPTER THREE

HUGH DUNCAN knew that as he drove slowly through the village of Little Soham he was an object of interest to many invisible eyes, and speculation upon many tongues.

It was not often that a Rolls went as far as the jetty. When cars of that sort came to Little Soham, they usually stopped at the upper end of the village and were catered for by the landlord of the Crown and Anchor.

But this stranger not only drove as far as the jetty. He continued right on to the landing, even though he found some difficulty in negotiating the long car through the narrow passage that separated two tumbledown wooden buildings.

He stopped about midway along the jetty, and, relaxing, lighted his pipe. From this point he had a clear view of the river, which, rather than the sea, forms the harbour of Little Soham.

The tide was out. On either side of the stream the mud-flats lay glistening in the morning sun. Directly across from the jetty was the "island," a long, low, sandy bank about half a mile wide that separated the fishing village from the North Sea. In order to reach the island, it was necessary to go down from the village about six miles and then cross a sand-bar.

On a far distant point of the island was a lighthouse and coastguard station. Nearer at hand, as far as the eye could see, were the saltings and marsh flats, the latter protected from the tides by high earthen embankments. Not a tree was in sight. It was the flat country of the wild-fowl.

From each side of the jetty the ground sloped away gradually to the beach, where several boats were pulled

up. Half a dozen men were pottering about them, and
although no head was raised, the man in the car knew he
was undergoing steady, if surreptitious, scrutiny.

But Duncan did not hasten to gratify their curiosity.
He knew the people of that part of the country. He knew
how suspicious they were of strangers and how clannishly
defensive against the least hint of inquiry upon the part
of authority.

He had come to Little Soham in search of the answers
to certain questions. If he were to find them he would
have to make his approach very warily. The least hint
that he was even remotely connected with the police, and
he would find himself up against a conspiracy of silence
that nothing would break.

It was not, then, until he had finished his pipe and lit
another that he leisurely climbed out of the car. Nor, even
then, did he hasten to make contact with the men on the
beach.

He strolled to the end of the jetty and appeared to be
admiring the wide sweep of the marsh flats that lay away
towards the sea. Then he strolled back, and finally
arrived at the side of the first boat at which one of the
fishermen was working.

The man was a big, beefy fellow, with a weather-red
face, and the slow, drawl of Suffolk. He had, too, the
natural courtesy of his kind.

Duncan talked to him for some minutes about his
calling and its hazards. He showed a deliberate ignorance
of conditions in this particular part, but soon gained the
other's respectful attention when he referred to other
portions of the coast, and in doing so drew comparison to
various places abroad.

Under cover of the conversation he was able to show
an interest in the boat and gear, and by the time he
moved on to the next there had travelled among the
fishermen the news that here was a stranger who had
just drifted into the village by chance with an hour or so
to idle away.

But if they were watchful of him, he noticed their every movement. There was one among them who caught his attention particularly.

This was a fellow who worked over a small motorboat which was hauled out at the very edge of the water. Like its owner, it stood out from the other craft by means of its smart appearance and speedy lines. It was obviously kept with the most meticulous care, and now, under the rubbing which was receiving, the brasswork was glistening like burnished gold under the sun.

The man himself was a handsome specimen of his type. He was well built, and, Duncan thought, very powerful. His hair was as black as jet, his skin of a southern European swarthiness rather than a Northern tan. His eyes were intensely blue, but set possibly a little too close together.

He replied quietly to Duncan's greeting and talked readily about his work. It seemed that the motorboat was used for running trippers up and down the river during the holiday time, and he confessed freely enough that this proved far more profitable than fishing.

Duncan thought the craft an exceptionally fine one to be put to such a purpose, and he guessed, that her speed would be high. But he said nothing of this. While he talked he was stealing glances at the tiller-handle with which, as well as the steering-wheel, the boat was equipped.

It might or might not have been new, for it was varnished like the rest of the interior. But there was a long gouge on one side of the tiller-post that looked as if it might have been caused by a very violent wrenching of some sort, and there was some peculiarity about the graceful curve of the handle that Duncan found familiar.

It was not, however, until he had invited the half a dozen men to accompany him the few yards to The Jolly Sailor for a beer that he was able to make the actual connection in his mind. Then all of a sudden it came to him. The tiller-handle had been trebly grooved on each side for a hand-grip, a refinement that none of the other tiller-handles showed but which was possessed by the broken one now in the hands of the police at Benham.

Duncan made himself congenial, and at the end of a quarter of an hour he was in possession of a piece of information which for private reasons he had not wished to get from Clark. This was the exact location of Dr. Grunevald's sanitorium. The question served, too, to provide the curious fishermen with a satisfactory reason for his being at Little Soham.

Two miles out of the village he drew up at the side of the road. From his pocket he took the letter which he had received that morning from Scotland Yard.

Inspector Pointer had enclosed the full dossier regarding the matter upon which Duncan was engaged, but in it he found no hint of anything that would give a clue to what Peel might have stumbled upon before his reports had ceased.

One thing, however, seemed to him to be strongly indicated. This was that a visit to Dr. Grunevald's sanitorium should be undertaken as his next step, for it was to this place that the son Of Sheik El Bakr had been brought and where presumably he was to be found. It was possible that he might be to say what had become of Peel.

From the spot where he had drawn up, Duncan could see the chimneys of a building which he now knew to be Dr. Grunevald's establishment, and although the angle was different, he knew, too, that they were those same chimneys which he had seen day before from the platform of the Martello Tower.

As he had told the chief-inspector in London, he knew the name of Dr. Grunevald well enough by repute. The doctor was a Swiss bacteriologist, whose treatment of nervous ailments was as fiercely denounced by one school of medical men as it was lauded and defended by another. It was, as Duncan understood it, a method of treatment by injection of a serum which was very costly to produce owing to the fact that it required five years to prepare.

Now, as he approached the large, well-kept estate, with its mellow old manor-house snug among trees, he realised that Dr. Grunevald must be a man of considerable means to carry out his arch work in such a remote spot.

Then he remembered the select patients who were received into the place for treatment. It was probable, he thought, that they paid highly for such surroundings, and the profit from the "home" might well go a long way to pay for the research work.

He found that in order to reach the front gate he must turn off a main road for about a hundred yards. He was just on the point of doing so when he saw in his driving mirror the figure of a motor-cyclist coming up at a rapid pace behind him. Even in the reflector he seemed to note something familiar about the figure, and as the other swung past him round the corner, and in passing smiled slightly, Duncan recognised him as one of the fishermen with whom he had talked at Little Soham—the one whose dark good looks had particularly attracted his attention.

Slung over the man's shoulder was a small canvas bag that bulged as if it might contain fish, and it seemed a perfectly natural thing for him to turn in at the gates of the big place just ahead. After all, fresh fish would be a frequent item on the diet-sheet of such an establishment, and Little Soham was the logical place to buy supplies.

Then Duncan also turned in through the wide gateway. As he approached the house along a winding drive, he caught another glimpse of the fisherman vanishing around the corner of the mansion towards the kitchen quarters.

Just before reaching the front portico, there was an opening through the oaks, revealing a lovely vista of gardens and parks.

Several persons were moving about or sitting in the sun. Evidently these were the resident patients. One of them, an elderly man, tall and upright with a white beard

as large as a spade was quite close to the drive, and as
Duncan caught sight of him he stopped the car quickly.

"Good-morning, Sir James."

He got out of the car and went towards the other, who
had paused and turned to regard him uncertainly.

"It is Sir James Pinder, isn't it?" queried Duncan.

"Yes; but who . . . why, it's Hugh Duncan!"

"Quite right, sir. I was sure it was you. I didn't expect
to see you here."

They shook hands. The eyes of Sir James were
twinkling.

"You thought I was done for? Well, I'm not. I believe
they've had me practically in my grave, but you can see
how wrong they are. I haven't been so fit for years."

Duncan remembered that nearly a year ago it had
been announced that Sir James Pinder, the eminent
explorer and noted authority on Middle-East archeology,
had suffered from a severe nervous breakdown. There
had followed rumours that he was in a state of feebleness
from which there was no chance of any real recovery. Yet
here he was, looking as he had just said, as fit as possible.

"You certainly look the picture of health," Duncan
agreed. "Is it this place that has done it?"

"Every bit. I've been here for nine months now. I'll do
a full year. Grunevald insists. He's a marvel, that man,
but you can't monkey with him. He disciplines us like a
lot of naughty children, but he gets results. Look at me.
I'm back to fifty again. What are you doing here, Duncan?
Have you some friend in residence?"

"No. As a matter of fact I happened to be down in this
part of the country and thought I would make inquiries of
the welfare of a young fellow from Arabia who has just
come to the place for treatment."

He sensed some swift and subtle change in the other's
manner. It was as if he stiffened, and then as quickly
relaxed. The impression was so fleeting that Duncan
could not be sure that it had actually been received.

"You ought to find Grunevald in his office," he heard Sir James say. "He was in the grounds a few minutes ago making his morning rounds, but I saw him going towards the house. By the way, don't tell any one about finding me so improved, there's a good fellow. I want to give the croakers a bit of a shock when I come out."

Duncan promised, and returned to the car. He finished his drive to the portico still puzzling over the indefinable change that had seemed to come over Sir James for a brief moment. It was almost as if the mention of the youth from Arabia had been unwelcome to him, or had startled him. But why? And why should he have immediately suppressed the feeling? If Duncan's instinct was right, then there was something here that he would very much like to understand. But how, he asked himself, could Sir James Pinder have anything to conceal?

The door was opened by a trim maid who took his card and asked him to follow her.

He stepped into a large sunny room that was very well-furnished as a combination of study and consulting-room. Even as he crossed the threshold, some one went out by a door on his left as he stood facing the interior. He caught a fleeting glimpse of a thick blue jersey and blue serge trousers caught round the ankles by spring clips. He was almost sure that it was the fisherman from Little Soham who had passed him on the road and entered the gates just ahead of him.

This he saw out of the corner of an eye. His direct gaze was upon the man who sat facing him behind a broad flat desk. He knew it could only be Dr. Grunevald.

The bacteriologist was a man of bulky torso, and long legs that were thrust straight out in the knee-opening, of the desk. He was distinctly handsome, with a fine intellectual face and bright quick eyes that needed no glasses. His brown hair and short, pointed beard were immaculately trimmed and brushed. He was so beautifully dressed in a light-grey suit as to be almost foppish. A monocle which must have been pure

affectation hung from a black cord, and at the moment he
was twisting it between long, white, sensitive fingers. He
looked, in fact, what he was, a prosperous, intellectual
scientist or professional man who was very sure of
himself, and whose weakness was possibly self-
adornment.

He greeted his visitor courteously enough but did not
rise. Duncan bowed and glanced towards his card, which
lay on the desk in front of the other.

"I hope I am not disturbing you, Dr. Grunevald, but I
happened to be near here, and thought I would stop to
ask after the welfare of one of your patients who has
recently arrived."

"Delighted!" interrupted Grunevald. "I shall be
pleased to accommodate you in any way possible. But I
cannot spare you much time just now. I am due to make
my morning rounds to those who are unable to leave their
rooms. Whom did you wish to know about?"

His voice was pleasantly low and agreeable to the ear.
He was smiling now, and had his head lifted inquiringly.

"I am interested in an Arab youth who has come to
England for your treatment, Dr. Grunevald—the son of
Sheik El Bakr of El Wejh."

"Ah, yes. He has only been with me a few days. I am
scarcely able to give an opinion yet. He is still resting and
under observation, you understand. I hope you will not
ask to see him, because he must receive no visitors for
some little time."

"Then I shall not do so, Dr. Grunevald. After all, as
long as I know he's getting on well—"

"Please sit down, Mr. Duncan. I do not ask you to
smoke as I do not allow it in this room. Now about this
youth, what can I tell you? That he will receive every
care? Yes. For how long must he remain? That is
impossible to say. But his father will, of course, receive
regular reports. It is a nuisance that his personal medical
advisor could not remain longer, but he will soon get used
to us."

The statement was a surprising one. There was nothing in Peel's report to show that the medical attendant—to whom he had referred several times —had left his charge after placing him in the sanatorium. Had Peel not known it? Or, if he had, why had he not mentioned it?

Duncan determined to lay a few more cards on the table.

"I will be frank with you, Dr. Grunevald. As a matter of fact, I have been asked in certain official quarters in London to inquire as to the well-being of this Arab youth. It is from a quarter that is taking a rather paternal interest in him, and while I was down here it was convenient for me to call. I did not know that his own medical attendant had left him."

"It was a surprise to me, I assure you. When he arrived I thought he would stay for some time. But he insisted that he must leave once he had seen his charge safely into my hands. I did my best to persuade him to change his plans, but it was useless."

"Has he returned to Arabia?"

"I do not know. He left here, that is all I can tell you."

Duncan spent another quarter of an hour or so with Dr. Grunevald. When he finally rose to take his leave, he had a feeling that the other had talked a great deal without saying anything.

But in no single instance could he put his finger on a flaw in the scientist's answers. He had been perfectly affable and appeared both quick and ready to respond.

Yet there was something very unsatisfactory in the whole interview. Dr. Grunevald stated that the young Arab had come into his care and was receiving every attention. He politely but firmly blocked Duncan's every approach to the subject of an interview with the patient.

There was, too, the surprising statement that the young man's medical attendant had left him. Duncan was sure that this was not known to Scotland Yard, even if it had been known to the missing Peel.

A final question occurred to him.

"How did the medical attendant leave?" he asked.

"I believe he ordered a car locally and drove to some railway station, but of that I cannot be certain as I was engaged when he left."

Duncan let it go at that. He thanked the other for his kindness, and found on opening the door that the maid was waiting to show him out.

He did not see Sir James Pinder again, although he drove slowly down the drive to the gate, searching keenly in every direction.

Other eyes than his were busy at the same time. Inside Dr. Grunevald's private room two people watched his departure, although only Grunevald would have been visible had Duncan still been in the room.

But a voice came from a large leather screen that enclosed one corner of the room. It was soon evident that this invisible person had been there during the whole interview.

"Is he driving away?"

Grunevald turned away from the window. "Yes, he's going down the drive now."

"Do you think he saw Frost?"

"Not enough to recognise him. In any case it doesn't matter. He couldn't guess what Frost was doing here. Frost knows enough to watch his step. You can come out now."

At this, a leaf of the screen swung aside and a man emerged from the hiding-place. He joined Grunevald at the window, and together they watched Duncan disappear at the lower end of the drive.

On reaching the road Duncan turned to the left. He knew that his shortest route back to Benham was the way he had come that morning. The turn was about two miles farther on, and then the distance would be about eight miles, for the road made a wide circle around the sandy expanse of little Sahara.

On the other hand, by keeping on past the turn and continuing for another couple of miles, he would reach the market town of Ockham. Here was the nearest railway station to Little Soham, one that would be used by any one going away by train from any part of the surrounding district. Inquiries at the railway station might tell him more of the departure of the medical attendant about whose movements Dr. Grunevald had been so vague.

It was getting on for twelve, too, and he decided that by the time he reached Ockham he could do with a spot of lunch. So he passed the turning for Benham, and a few minutes later was entering the market town.

He drove slowly along the narrow main street, then turned sharply to the left. He was making for The Dog and Pheasant, and just before reaching it was compelled to pull up entirely, to allow a large red-and-yellow tinker's caravan to negotiate the difficult turn out of the inn-yard into the road.

He was just moving out again when a motorcyclist emerged and came at a reckless pace towards him. The fellow flashed past, speeding hard, but not so quickly that Duncan could not see him plainly. And he knew that the other had seen him, for their eyes met squarely for a brief instant.

It was Frost, the cycling fisherman from Little Soham. But this time the man had no smile on his lips.

Duncan manoeuvred the big car into the inn-yard and climbed out. He entered by the side door, and on his way to the bar parlour had to pass through a small sitting-room.

It was there that he received another surprise. Sitting in a chair before an apology for a fire, hunched up as if he were feeling miserably cold although the day was now fine and warm outside, was an individual of swarthy skin.

He was dressed in a suit of stiff black serge and wore hideous pointed-toed boots of cheap yellow leather. But there his outward deference to European dress practically

finished. His head was swathed in a soiled turban or,
rather, head-dress, of the sort worn by the Wahabi Arabs.

CHAPTER FOUR

THE fellow looked so forlorn and unhappy that Duncan was almost tempted to speak to him, but for the moment he passed on.

Crossing the hall, he entered the public bar in search of the landlord, whom he found polishing glasses behind the counter. He made arrangements to lunch in half an hour. He had intended questioning the inn-keeper about the Arab customer whom he had seen in the parlour, but decided to defer that for a more favourable opportunity, as there were others in the tap-room.

Instead, he set off on foot for the railway station, which was only a few minutes' walk. The stationmaster was away for his dinner, but he got hold of a porter, and using the persuasion of a little palm oil was soon receiving answers to his questions.

None of them cleared up the matter about which he was curious. The porter remembered a dark foreigner well enough, but not as leaving Ockham. It was as an incoming passenger that he placed him, and was quite positive that he was still, in the town, for he had seen him at The Dog and Pheasant.

Duncan described briefly the man in the inn parlour. The porter assured him that this was the man he meant, and when Duncan insisted that another man of similar hue had left by train, the porter shook his head energetically.

"No, sir, I haven't seen any one like that but him."

"Neither arriving nor leaving?"

"No, sir. Neither way."

"It is possible that the man I want to find sent some luggage on to the station in advance. Would you be so good as to make sure."

"I don't know of any, sir, but come along with me and look for yourself."

The small collection of bags and boxes yielded nothing. So, after a thorough canvass of all the possibilities, Duncan was forced to the conclusion that he would find no clue to the movements of the dark-skinned medical attendant at Ockham railway station; which, considering what Dr. Grunevald had told him, was rather curious—and baffling.

Duncan gave it up and returned to the inn.

When he had finished his lunch he lighted his briar, and, being alone in the small room, decided on a test. The entry of the landlord at that moment to see how he was getting on gave him the idea.

"It has been a most delightful lunch," Duncan told him with a smile, "but there is just one thing lacking."

"And what is that, sir? I hope the girl has looked after you properly."

"Oh, yes, indeed, she has been most attentive. What I was thinking was that a spot of nice brandy would top things off beautifully."

The landlord rubbed his chin and gazed out of the window.

"As a matter of fact, I believe I might find you something of the sort, sir. I'll see what I can do."

When he was gone Duncan reflected that Inspector Clark would not have been able to approach the landlord in this fashion. He was putting a sudden theory of his to the test, and the way the landlord had received his suggestion promised an interesting result.

The landlord entered the room a few minutes later bearing a tray on which was a bottle and a crystal goblet of thin glass. The bottle was filled with a liquid of a golden-brown shade and bore no label. The glass was of much better quality than one would have expected to have seen in this country inn.

"You try a drop of this, sir, with my compliments," he said affably. "I think you'll find it nice bit of stuff."

Duncan held the goblet between his hands until the glass was warm. Then he poured in a small quantity of the cognac. He bent his head to inhale the bouquet, then, with a nod to the other, lifted the goblet and tilted it.

He took only a sip, which he allowed to nip slowly over his tongue and take a smooth course past his palate. It was as smooth as liquid sunshine, and Duncan needed no more than that to tell him that a brandy of this age and vintage had never found its way into the country inn through the usual prosaic channels; so that when, a quarter of an hour later, after another of the seductive liqueurs, he drove out of the inn-yard, he had made up his mind very definitely that he was going to put his theory to a further test. For the present he would make no inquiries about the Easterner in the parlour.

He must get back to Benham as quickly as possible.

His quickest way now was, he knew, to turn back till he reached the road by which he had half-intended going when he left Dr. Grunevald's sanatorium. This would take him round that estate and would at the same time avoid a near approach to Little Soham.

It was just on three when Duncan left Ockham. The lovely day had changed with the banking of ominous clouds to the south-west. A chill wind was blowing, and it looked as if it would not be long before the clouds covered the whole of the sky, bringing rain with them.

But Duncan's mind was on neither the weather nor the purpose that had taken him to Ockham. He was thinking rather of the forlorn-looking Arab he had seen crouching over the miserable fire at the inn. He was trying to guess what possible reason could have brought him to this out-of-the-way part of England. His very appearance was sufficient to arouse suspicion. Yet something of considerable importance must have induced him to face a climate and conditions so utterly alien to those he had always known.

What? Was it some reason that might be linked up with that other Arab who was in the care of Dr.

Grunevald—the son of Sheik El Bakr? Or with the one of the same hue, if not race, whose body had been found in the sand near the Martello Tower?

So engrossed was he in these cogitations that he took the turning into the heath road almost mechanically. It was only when beyond the trees he saw an extensive roof and many chimneys that he realised he was at the back of the sanatorium.

Just ahead of him now the road dipped into a valley, where it wound through thick woods and crossed a stream before rising to a ridge some two miles beyond.

The clouds had swept across the sky so quickly that a dark canopy now covered all the heavens and the branches of the trees creaked as they swayed,

It was the chill of this wind that caused Duncan to slow down while he closed the windscreen and side-windows, which he had opened for ventilation.

And it was this that was to save his life within the next few minutes, for, as he started the car again, there broke upon him, without the slightest warning, a determined and savage attack.

It came from the left concealment of the wood. The staccato racketing of what Duncan's trained ear took to be a sub-machine-gun could easily be heard as a hail of bullets spattered against glass and bodywork.

So surprised was he by this sudden outburst that for the first few moments he kept the same pace, concerned more with noting if the bullet-proof glass was as effective as he had been led to believe, or whether it would splinter under fire at such close range.

But the windows held. Here and there the force of the impact would paint a spider's web upon the side-windows, which were in the direct line of fire, but not one penetrated the glass. Realising at last that even that protection might not stand for long, he accelerated hard.

The car took up the challenge smoothly and purposefully. He flashed past the line of danger and was gone, a shower of bullets pattering after him.

Then they ceased. At the bottom of the valley, where a small bridge spanned the stream, he drew up and got out. He cast a cautious look around. A blackbird broke into noisy protest and went fussing off along the hedgerow, warning every other wild creature of his presence. But, with that one exception, there wasn't sight or sound of any living thing. It seemed incredible that only a few moments before a stream of bullets could have been pouring out of that dark and silent wood.

But the multitude of marks on the car were proof enough of the reality of it all. Either one or two rapid-fire guns had done that damage, or at least half a dozen automatic pistols held in different hands. Duncan was inclined to think that the former was the right surmise. There had been a continuity about the stream that indicated a single source.

He speculated upon the chances of taking his own revolver from the side pocket of the car and walking back up the hill. But common sense told him that if the road were still being watched to do so would be to achieve as rapid a death as one could desire. And if, as seemed probable, the person or persons who had launched that murderous attack were well away by now, he would still achieve nothing. The attack had been no haphazard shooting by some lunatic.

He re-entered the car, and drove on. While keeping a careful look-out, he tried to find an explanation for this amazing episode which, but for the fact that the car was bullet-proof, would have meant that he would have been riddled through and through.

CHAPTER FIVE

YOUNG Prince Faud, son of the Sheik El Bakr of El Wejh, and lineal descendant of the Prophet Mohammed, was puzzled and uneasy.

He was at a loss to understand why his friend and confidant, Dr. Raas, had left him so unceremoniously. He had not given the slightest hint that he was going. Indeed, the matter had not been discussed as a possibility. What, then, did it mean?

The young man, tall even for the ruling house of Nedj, looked out upon the lovely English park that lay beneath him. It would have been difficult to picture anything less disturbing than this peaceful scene, and yet Prince Faud was filled with an uneasiness that he could not dispel.

Why had Raas gone without a word? What business could be of such an urgent nature that he must steal away like some desert bandit? If the prince had not been so anxious he would have been angry; for, friend or no, Dr. Raas was in his personal service.

But he could not believe that Raas had acted as an entirely free agent. He knew that his father, Sheik El Bakr, had given Raas very definite instructions. His father, Raas and himself knew that the object of this visit to England was not that he might receive certain medical treatment. In reality, he was as fit as the hard desert life could make him. A very different purpose lay behind the journey, and here in this remote place, where the first cautious move was to have been made, Raas had vanished without leaving the slightest clue.

In his dilemma Faud was uncertain of what he should do. He was supposed to have come to this sanatorium to be treated for an obscure nervous ailment. The matter had been arranged by his father before he left Arabia, and the medical arrangements had been left to Raas. It was Raas who had talked with Dr. Grunevald and his assistant on his arrival; and it was he who should have been at hand to act as buffer between his charge and the other physicians while the real purpose of his visit was being pressed forward.

Prince Faud could not conceive of Raas deserting him. The man was thoroughly loyal. If he had disappeared in such a fashion it was through the machinations of some one else. If this view was correct then it could mean only one thing—some one knew the secret purpose of their presence in England.

It was the first time in his life that young Prince Faud had been called upon to make a major decision. Hence he shied away from the necessity like an unbroken horse. Yet he knew that it was vital to take some action without delay.

Should he send a cable to his father asking his advice? He knew that the Sheik El Bakr was engaged in desert hostilities with the Sheereef of Kaijh, and that it might be many days, even weeks, before such a message would reach him.

Should he make further inquiries of Dr. Grunevald? He had already asked in that direction. He had not seen Dr. Grunevald himself, but that gentleman's assistant had been sent to inform him that Dr. Raas had left the place with no more explanation than that he had been suddenly called away.

It occurred to him that he might pack up and do as Raas seemed to have done. But he knew that was impossible. He had a duty in this place and it must be carried through.

But how to make the necessary contact without Raas? It would mean disclosing his interest in a certain individual, and that was a danger which he had been strictly warned to avoid. Then what?

It was something he saw in the park which enabled him to decide, though this decision meant disobeying those very instructions. But, he told himself, circumstances warranted it. After all, his father could not have anticipated such a dilemma as this.

Strolling about the park were several patients or inmates of the place. It was the sight of one of these, the very person with whom he had come down to make secret contact, which decided him what to do. That person was Sir James Pinder, the noted authority on the Middle East.

Prince Faud turned away from the window and walked across the comfortably furnished sitting room to the bell. He rang and then sat down.

The summons was answered promptly by a man in a blue suit cut so severely that it looked like a uniform. Prince Faud spoke to him in fair English.

"I wish to see the Dr. Grunevald," he told the man. "You will take him my compliments and tell him my desire."

"Very good, Your Highness."

The man's manner was perfectly respectful and natural, the exact deference he should have shown to a resident as distinguished as Prince Faud. The whole atmosphere of the place inside and out, the complete freedom of the patients, everything, was just what it should have been in an establishment of this sort. Anything sinister seemed utterly alien to such surroundings, and yet the young Arab could no more dissipate an uneasy feeling that gripped him than he could push back the clouds moving up from the south.

It was not Dr. Grunevald who appeared. Instead, it was a tall individual whom Prince Faud had met the previous day and whom he knew as Dr. Grunevald's assistant, Dr. Harrison.

He was a strong-featured man of early middle age, clean-shaven, whereas Dr. Grunevald was whiskered, but quite as faultlessly dressed and as suave of manner.

He bowed and smiled an apology.

"Dr. Grunevald is so sorry that he cannot attend upon Your Highness at the moment," he said smoothly, "but he

is engaged upon some important treatment. He asks me
to say that he will be pleased to wait upon Your Highness
presently if you so wish. In the meantime I am entirely at
Your Highness's service."

Prince Faud inclined his head slightly. He had
watched closely and listened attentively, but there was
nothing at which he could cavil.

"Have you anything to tell me about my attendant,
Dr. Raas?"

"I regret, Your Highness, that there is nothing. If it is
your wish we can make inquiries in London, of course."

"No. It doesn't matter. But I am bored without his
company."

"I shall be only too happy to do anything in my power
to relieve Your Highness of boredom, and I am sure Dr.
Grunevald is equally anxious to do so. If Your Highness
would care to walk in the grounds it would not interfere
with the treatment which Dr. Grunevald might decide
upon. The first weeks are always rather trying. If Your
Highness would meet some of the other guests—"

"That is exactly in my mind. On the first day of our
arrival Raas saw a gentleman in the grounds whom he
believed he had seen before. If he was right, then this
gentleman is one well known to my father, and it would
give me pleasure to talk with him."

"Your Highness can give me his name?"

"Sir James Pinder. He has travelled very extensively
in Arabia, and it was my father's pleasure to show him
some small attention."

"But of course. Sir James Pinder is our most
distinguished authority on the history and archaeology of
Arabia. It was stupid of me not to think of that before. I
shall be delighted to take any message to him or to
arrange a meeting."

"I should be obliged if you would inquire if it would be
agreeable for him to visit me here—if not to-day, then
another time."

"I shall go at once."

With that Dr. Harrison bowed himself out, and with the closing of the door each of the two men thought he had so cleverly achieved his purpose that the other did not suspect there was any thing to suspect. One was right. One was wrong.

Prince Faud congratulated himself that he was making contact with Sir James Pinder in a way that even Dr. Raas could not have bettered. He was wrong.

Dr. Harrison believed that he had led up to same point without the other having the faintest idea that it was for this he had been playing since his arrival. He was right.

When a message reached Sir James Pinder that Dr. Grunevald sent his compliments and would be obliged if he could spare him a few minutes in his office, the archaeologist was already on his way to the house. Like all the other residents who were taking the air, he had been warned by an attendant that a storm was approaching rapidly.

He smiled a ready assent when he heard that His Highness Prince Faud, who had just arrived as a patient, had expressed a wish to meet him.

"Of course, my dear doctor. It will be a pleasure. I know his father, who showed me many kindnesses when I was in Arabia. When does he wish the meeting to be?

"Now, if you are agreeable. His personal attendant has left and he is, I fear, finding it somewhat dull. It would be a great kindness if you would break his ennui."

A few minutes later found Sir James being presented to the young Arabian in the latter's sitting-room. Dr. Harrison had taken it upon himself to conduct Sir James personally, and he was, therefore, a witness to the warm embrace with which the two met.

But neither his eye, keenly watchful, nor his ear, sharply attentive, saw or heard anything that could tell him if this interview was as unexpected as the two would have him believe.

That did not worry him unduly. He intended to follow all that passed during the meeting with no risk of discovery, and it was in order to do so without loss of time that he bowed himself out and closed the door.

He found Dr. Grunevald seated at the desk in his office. When he had closed the door he locked it. "Are you ready?"

Dr. Grunevald rose. His patients would have been surprised to watch the noted specialist during the next few minutes. He followed his colleague behind the large screen which had been in evidence during the visit of the fisherman from Little Soham.

The area it enclosed formed almost a small room. It contained a desk, a chair and a glass cabinet. One might surmise that it was used as a dispensing corner on occasion.

At the moment, however, it was being put to a very different use. On the desk lay two sets of earphones. One of these Dr. Harrison handed to Grunevald; the other pair he fitted over his own head. Then, while the one took the chair and the other eased himself on to the desk, there was silence as they listened to the sounds that reached them, sounds that were being conveyed through the hidden microphone in the sitting-room where Sir James Pinder sat with Prince Faud.

Dr. Harrison had a working knowledge of modern Arabic, both Syrian and Egyptian. He expected the talk between Sir James Pinder and the young Arab to be in English, but if by any remote chance they were to use Arabic, he told himself that he would be able to follow what was being said.

He was mistaken. What came to him was a meaningless jumble which he found quite impossible to understand. Nor was Grunevald able to be of any assistance. Both men recognised a word here and there, but each had only the barest knowledge of the classical Arabic that is used in Central Arabia.

Nevertheless, they continued to sit with the earphones clamped about their heads until the last word was spoken and they could hear the closing of the door as Sir James took his departure.

Then, however, Harrison tore the earphones from his head, and rose with an oath.

"If I can't get it one way, I'll have it another," he was storming when Grunevald held up his hand.

"Listen."

Through the windows, which were open at the top, came a rapid succession of sounds, faint in the distance. They lasted for no more than a matter of seconds, and one might have thought they came from a motor-cycle that was passing by some part of the estate. But, then, again, they might also be attributed to the racketing of some fast-shooting weapon such as a machine-gun or automatic rifle.

Whatever the genesis, the brief outburst was sufficient to cause Harrison to push aside a leaf of the screen and make for the door with long strides. He might or might not have been surprised to learn that at that moment Hugh Duncan was alive and driving along the road that ran at the back of the estate.

CHAPTER SIX

DUNCAN was in a dilemma as he drove on to Benham.

What should he tell the local inspector? He preferred not to make any explanation yet regarding the cause of the damage to his car, for that would mean going into details about the determined attempt to assassinate him.

On the other hand, Inspector Clark would be blind indeed if he did not see the bullet marks on the body and the "spider-webs" where many shots had struck the splinter-proof glass.

It was when he remembered that his assistant should by now be at Benham that a solution, temporary at least, came to him. Peter would, of course, proceed straight to the local inn. He would probably report to the local police station and then hang about until he heard from or saw Duncan. Even if Inspector Clark suggested that he should take up his quarters at the cottage, Peter would not accept the invitation.

This would give Duncan an excuse to leave the inspector's cottage and join the lad at the inn. When his mission in Suffolk had seemed to be no more than a routine inquiry on behalf of Scotland Yard, it did not matter about accepting the hospitality of the local inspector, but since his interview with Dr. Grunevald and the mysterious attack upon him, Duncan felt that he wanted more freedom of action than would be possible as the inspector's guest.

Therefore, on entering the main street he drove right past the police station and, turning in at the yard beside the inn, ran the car into a lock-up garage. He was crossing the yard when Peter came out of a side door. Their greeting was casual. Duncan found that the lad had only provisionally engaged a room, but a short talk with the landlord resulted in two bedrooms and a sitting-room being placed at their disposal. At this time of the year few persons found their way to Benham, and the two detectives had the inn to themselves, a circumstance which—in conjunction with the convenient situation of their rooms on the ground floor of the garden wing—was to prove useful in more ways than one.

"I suppose you've been along to the police station?" said Duncan as soon as they were alone.

"Yes. I thought I'd better, since you said you were staying with the local inspector. What's up, sir?"

"I don't know yet, Peter, but I think we are in the way of turning up something interesting."

"About this bloke whose body you found?"

"Possibly. What have you been told?"

"The sergeant in charge said you had found a body out on Little Sahara, that it was a case of murder, and that the victim was some unidentified foreigner."

"That about describes it."

"But how did you find it, sir? Did you stumble upon it by accident? He also said you'd uncovered some smuggled brandy."

"Listen and I'll tell you. I'll also tell you about something else I have found, and about which the local police know nothing so far. More than that, I have had a most interesting experience this afternoon."

He stuffed his pipe and gave Peter a brief but full outline of all that had happened since his arrival in Benham. The mysterious attack seemed to impress Peter.

"I suppose it was intended for you, sir?"

"I should say it had been devised solely and entirely for my benefit."

"But how could they know you were going to pass along that road—at that time?"

"They couldn't be sure, for the simple reason that I didn't decide to do so until I left Ockham."

"Then I don't see how it was staged."

"Don't you see that it means my movements must have been under close surveillance? If, for example, I had not returned by that road, it is possible that an attack would have been made at another spot, provided that conditions were favourable. On the other hand, the attack may have been postponed. But I feel certain that some one was advised when I left Ockham, and figuring that there was a good chance I would drive to Benham by the shortest route, was able to set the stage for my passing."

"But who would do it?"

"Ah! There you touch on something more obscure. Let us say for the moment only that it was some one who had very strong motives for eliminating me as quickly as possible—but from what?"

"I'm hanged if I know, unless it was something to do with the bloke you found in the sand."

"It might have been. On the other hand, we must remember that I have not yet discovered what brought me down into Suffolk."

"You mean Detective-Sergeant Peel?"

"Exactly."

Peter gave a low whistle.

"I didn't think of that. You don't suspect that anything has happened to him, do you? I mean, if he is around, he probably has his own reasons for lying doggo."

"Possibly; but I would call your attention to two things."

"What are they?"

"First, although I have been scouting about for a couple of days over the same ground where one would expect Peel to be found, I have not seen a trace of him. Secondly, there is a note-book which I believe to be his property which I found in the sand at the Martello Tower along with the contraband brandy."

"Are you sure it is his?"

Duncan thrust a hand into an inner pocket and took out the small black book which he had scraped out of the

sand in the upper room at the Martello Tower. He opened
it, and then passed it across to Peter.

"Take a squint at those entries. If Peel didn't write
them, who did? They were certainly put down by some
one who was following the movements of the young Arab
whom Peel had been told off to watch. But I don't think
we need doubt the ownership. The entries agree in detail
with the copies of Peel's reports which were in the dossier
Pointer sent me, and the writing tallies with a letter of
Peel's to the chief-inspector, which he handed to me."

"Then how did the note-book get there?"

"A most interesting speculation, Peter. Let me show
you something else. Last evening, before turning in, I
spent some time over these rather cryptic entries. I
believe I was able to discover a meaning that seems
reasonable. I should say they are, not really, in cipher,
but are just disjointed abbreviations which had sufficient
meaning for Peel, but which he felt would be no more
than a confusing jumble to any one else"

While he was speaking, he was turning the pages, and
now he indicated the curious entries that had occupied
his special attention.

"You see here, on the first page, Peter, we have, A.F. .
. . L.S. . . . 19—18 n.g.' Now, turning over, you see, on the
next page, 'A.F. . . . p.b. . . . 40 knots.' And, on the third,
'Fr. Cr. . . . camouf (?) . . , . Thurs. (?) . . . . A.F. (?).' That
finishes them."

"Well, some of it seems clear enough, sir. There is this
'40 knots.' That looks like the speed of a boat."

"Quite so, And I think we can take it that 'camouf' is
an abbreviation for camouflage, while 'Thurs' should
mean Thursday."

Peter grinned.

And 'n.g.' means no good."

Instead of smiling again, Duncan gave him sharp
look.

"By jove, I wonder if you're right! It might be just the
way Peel would jot down items with that meaning. Let

me give you my understanding of this from the beginning."

He took the book from Peter and began at the first page.

"Now look here. We find these initials 'A.F' on three different occasions. They refer, I believe, to some place or persons, because they are written in capitals. Well, I have made a close study of my own Government survey map for this district and I can find no place of any sort with those initials, though that does not necessarily mean that one does not exist, or even that the initials refer to such."

"Sounds reasonable, just the same."

"On the other hand, I have been able to identify 'F' with that of more than one family widely settled throughout the district. The name of one such family is 'Frost,' and I have further made the interesting, if possibly unimportant, discovery that the first name of the fisherman who caught my special attention at Little Soham, and whom I saw later at Dr. Grunevald's sanatorium at Ockham, is known as Abel Frost. Again, it seemed to me that these two initials 'L.S.' might be taken to indicate Little Soham."

Peter grinned again, this time admiringly.

"This bird Abel Frost seems to be popping up a good deal, sir."

"My guess may be wrong. Just the same, here in the second entry we have the same initials, then 'p.b.,' and lastly '40 knots.' That, at least, is plain enough."

"And 'p.b.' might be short for pub."

"I think it is more likely to mean power-boat." The grin vanished from Peter's face.

"My aunt! I bet you're right. 'A.F. . . . p.b. 40 knots.' Abel Frost . . . power-boat . . . 40 knots. That makes sense, anyway, or would, if this fellow Frost owned such a boat."

"I can tell you that he does, and that I should not be in the least surprised to learn that it is capable of the high speed of forty knots."

"Why should Peel be interested in that?"

"We don't know yet. But let us follow the thing through. Here is a third entry: we have the initials 'Fr. . . . Cr.' to begin with. Now I told you that I had made a very thorough examination of the Government survey map covering this area, and, although I did not find any place of two names beginning with the initials A.F., I did find something of two names that could be abbreviated to the 'Fr. Cr.'"

Peter's low whistle was a question.

"Not far from here," went on Duncan, "and cutting through the marshes through Little Soham, are several creeks which are the haunt of wild fowl—very lonely country they drain."

"I know that."

"Well, one of those creeks is known as French Creek. As a matter of fact, it empties into the river some distance below Little Soham. Now let us take the next item."

"'Camouf,' with an interrogation mark after it."

"Exactly. I am inclined to agree with you that it means 'camouflage' or 'camouflaged.' The interrogation mark might indicate that the person who made the note was not certain whether the word applied to something definite or not."

"Sounds reasonable."

"I hope so. Then we come to 'Thurs.' Thursday seems the most likely interpretation, for we must remember that we are not solving a cipher but what we think are abbreviations. We also find an interrogation mark after this word. We can surmise that the writer was not quite sure in his mind whether Thursday was the correct day for something or other; or it might have been that whatever incident or object had caught his attention was connected with the day Thursday."

"To-day is Thursday," remarked Peter.

"That had already occurred to me. Now, finally, we come again to the initials 'A.F.' Whatever they may mean, they are certainly closely identified with all three entries."

"Then what do you make of the whole thing, Chief?"

"I'll give you a skeleton theory, Peter. I suggest that the person who wrote these notes was interested for some special reason in another person whose initials are A.F. I suggest further that that person is to be found connected in some way with Little Soham, and also with a power-boat that is capable of a speed of forty knots, and that there is a further connection with French Creek with something or other which is suspected of camouflage and with a Thursday. As for the numbers '19-18' followed by 'n.g.,' I must confess that so far I have been unable to give them a definite meaning. On the other hand, an idea is working in my mind, and as soon as possible I shall put it to a test."

"But why should Peel be interested in this mysterious bloke and his doings, if he were down here to look after Prince Faud? Surely the two can't be connected?"

"If we assume that Peel stumbled upon contraband brandy, he may have heard something that we don't know but which he considered most important. Furthermore, the murder of that fellow I found may have some connection with the activities of the smugglers, though I must say I shall be very surprised if it is a direct one. These fellows along here regard smuggling as a justifiable sport; they would regard murder in a very different light."

"Then what is our next step? Will you tell all this to the local police?"

"By no means. I shall let them get on with investigating the murder. You and I are going to make our own inquiries along different channels. And because I have a theory about certain incidents that have occurred we shall make a start to-night."

"Where are we going? Into Little Soham?"

"We are going to make a start some miles from there—in the wooded country on the other side of Ockham."

CHAPTER SEVEN

THEY slipped out of Benham early in the evening.

Duncan had seen Inspector Clark and explained that he thought it better to move along to the inn with Peter. He had also given him a brief, colourless description of his doings during the day, indicating that he had some reason to believe that he would soon be able to throw some light on the identity of the murdered man.

But he gave no hint of his intentions to leave Benham that same evening. Nor did he himself know what a night of perilous adventure and uncertain ending it was to be.

No one saw them as they took their departure. No one would have expected to see Duncan astride the pillion of Peter's motor-cycle; indeed, it had been no little surprise to the lad himself when Duncan took his seat on it for their journey.

It wouldn't be the first time the powerful machine had been used on such business, and because of this possible need, it was equipped with a large muffler that effectively silenced the exhaust until it was no more than a whisper.

Under ordinary conditions nothing would have pleased Peter more than to have let the machine all out and if possible give Duncan a ride he would remember. But the present circumstances forbade any such delights, and it was at a steady thirty miles only that the purring monster slid through the night across the lonely heath.

Peter had received the briefest instructions from Duncan.

"Drive across the heath to Ockham," he had said; "then right through Ockham to the moor. You can't miss the road, and in any event I shall be along to keep you right. Keep your eyes open for a gipsy wagon or caravan painted red and yellow. I'll know it if I see it, and will tell you. But you are not to stop. Keep straight on till I give you a sign."

They passed along the road where Duncan had been attacked, but he did not indicate the spot to Peter. That was over and done with, and his mind was on what might lie ahead. He had evolved a theory that could account for certain things which had cropped up during the day, and he wanted to lose no time in putting it to the test.

Even though the pace was what Peter would describe as a "crawl," they were approaching Ockham in less than half an hour after leaving Benham. The main street was in darkness but for a feeble light that drifted out from two or three shops.

Almost immediately they were in the open country again, and, with the exception of a secondary road, the way led to the north.

Now Duncan leant even closer to Peter so that he could see over his shoulder. The powerful headlights cut through the darkness ahead in a brilliant, widening cone that revealed every gradient and dip as if by day, that rolled back the night against the trees on each side as against a gloomy back-drop.

It was when they were some four miles out of Ockham and the country was becoming steadily more wild in appearance that an object caught their eye. A gipsy caravan was drawn up on the verge, and in the bright light of the headlamps they could see that it was painted a gaudy red and yellow. A horse grazed a short distance from it, but the end door of the wagon was closed, and as they flashed past Duncan could see no sign of human life.

Half a mile farther on he poked Peter in the ribs. "Pull up at a likely spot."

Peter slowed down. Scarcely had he done so when on the right the beam revealed the opening to a track that led into the wood. It was cut by deep wagon-ruts, but Peter managed to negotiate the motor-cycle between the ruts until they were twenty or thirty yards inside the woods. Then he cut off the engine.

"This do, sir?"

"Couldn't be better. I'll give you a hand and we'll wheel the machine out of sight. Then douse the lights."

They pushed the motor-cycle over a bumpy course until it could stand completely hidden; then Peter switched off the lights and they stood in complete darkness.

"What now?" he whispered. "I take it that caravan we passed is what you wanted, sir?"

"Yes. I've got to have a look inside."

"Supposing there is some one there?"

"Then we've got to dispose of them. Come on, we'll follow the road some way, then, take to the woods again. Keep your eye out for dogs—these fellows often have a mangy cur or two, as you know."

They moved out to the main road again, and now that their eyes were becoming accustomed to the darkness found they could proceed easily enough without the aid of a torch, for the black tunnel of the trees showed faintly light where the sky was now spangled with stars.

They proceeded cautiously. Duncan knew that the passing of a motor-cycle or car would not be likely to arouse suspicion as the road was a thoroughfare to link Ockham with the main Norwich-Ipswich road, but pedestrians along that lonely path at this time of night would be sure to come under close scrutiny if they were observed by any one in the caravan.

They were still some distance from their objective when Duncan drew up. Against the black wall of the trees they could distinguish nothing of the caravan; but when they stood very still and quiet they could hear the slight movements of the horse.

No light showed. No dog gave tongue. Duncan touched Peter's arm and moved cautiously along the grass. Nearer and nearer they drew, until at last they could just distinguish the dim bulk of the wagon, now only a few yards distant.

They paused again; they could still hear the horse as he muzzled the grass. There was, too, the intermittent sound of metal on wood that Duncan guessed correctly was the ring on the hobble as the animal moved. But still no chink of light showed from the caravan. If the owner were within, he must either be asleep or, sitting in the dark.

That the latter was a possibility they both knew, and for this reason they did not discard their former caution as they crept on once more.

They were standing so close to the wagon that their shoulders were touching the structure, when suddenly the horse gave a loud snort, and the noisy rattle of the hobble-ring followed.

They flattened themselves against the wheel and stood still, scarcely breathing. The horse began munching again, the hobble-ring rattled slightly, and Duncan and Peter moved forward until, on edging round the side of the caravan, they reached the steps that led up to the door.

Duncan drew Peter close, so that he could breathe a warning in his ear.

"Get down and stay there. Keep your revolver handy. I'm going inside. If anything breaks suddenly you'll know what to do."

Peter pressed his arm to let him know that he understood. Then while the other slipped up the steps, he crouched down till he was in under the tail of the wagon.

Beyond the first slight noises when Duncan mounted the steps, he heard scarcely a sound for some minutes. Now and then, the tiniest hint of movement or contact would reach his ear, and this told him that Duncan was busy upon his purpose. But it was not until he heard a stealthy scraping sound immediately over his head that he knew Duncan had forced the lock and was now inside the caravan.

As a matter of fact, Duncan had found entry much more difficult than he had expected. A brief moment had been sufficient for his fingers to find the keyhole that was situated beside the handle, and this bolt he had forced back swiftly and easily, but when he turned the handle the door had still remained fast. He knew at once that the owner had taken more than usual pains to safeguard his wheeled dwelling, and while this circumstance told Duncan that the job was going to take longer, it also seemed to show that the owner was actually absent.

He knew enough about gipsies to guess that the first lock was no more than a flimsy blind, while the second would be much more intricate and much more carefully concealed.

He was right. He finally located it behind a cunningly contrived disc of steel high up in the frame. It was a good lock, but under his expert manipulation it soon yielded.

He stepped inside swiftly and closed the door. He knew that Peter was guarding the rear, so he could give all his faculties to what lay ahead. With his automatic in one hand and his torch in the other, he sent a beam of light travelling about the interior. While it was more or less what he had expected to find, it was filled so substantially that he knew a considerable sum of money was represented.

There was a curtain about half-way along that divided the caravan in two. This was drawn, and he left it for a moment. He noted, too, that the shutters were closed tight over each small window in the side.

The place seemed to be used as a kitchen and living quarters, while all about the wall and floor were piles of tin and ironware such as would form the tinkers' stock-in-trade.

A small iron stove still glowed hot—proof that the owner had been present not long since—and realising that he might well find the fellow fast asleep beyond the curtain, Duncan decided to investigate without further delay.

He tiptoed along until he could thrust one hanging aside. Focusing the light, he found himself looking into a most comfortably furnished place.

Against one wall was a bunk, neatly made up, and with no form showing in it. Beneath the window on the other side was a small table flap that could be held up by wall braces or let down flush with the wall. There was a gaily-coloured carpet on the floor. The walls, ceiling and supports were painted in brilliant reds and yellows, and against the front end, filling the whole available space from side to side and forming the only untidy note in the whole place, was a heap of heavy blankets and rugs, the sort, one would imagine, that the owner would bring into use for himself and the horse in cold and in wet weather.

Duncan reflected, however, that the pile looked somewhat voluminous to contain coverings for that purpose alone. It was not this alone, though, which caused him to investigate it more closely. It was because up to now the pile appeared the most likely hiding-place within the caravan for what he was seeking. For he had no doubt at all that this was the same tinker's wagon that he had seen coming out of the inn-yard at Ockham.

He put out his electric torch and moved forward until by bending he could touch the heap. Then, taking care not to disturb the coverings more than necessary, he delved into it until his groping hands encountered a hard object. It did not take long for his searching fingers to discern the shape and size of the object as just about what he had hopes to find.

Now he brought the torch into use again, and separating the coverings until he could bring the beam to bear on the object underneath, he peered at what he had discovered. And now he could be sure that his theory had been sound, for not only could he see one but could almost distinguish the curve of a second cask exactly similar to those he had found the previous afternoon in the upper room of the Martello Tower on Little Sahara, with the same characters and the port name of Rotterdam carved in the head of the first.

He readjusted the coverings carefully and backed away. He was quite human enough to find no little satisfaction in his discovery. On first seeing the red and yellow caravan coming out of the inn-yard at Ockham, he had told himself that here was an excellent means of getting contraband distributed about the country without arousing suspicion. Who travelled more widely than the gipsies? Who were more eager to earn a fat profit at that sort of game than the same people? And what sort of vehicle could travel across Little Sahara and cause less comment than a tinker's caravan?

From the moment he had noticed those parallel tracks in the sand outside the tower, Duncan had been satisfied that some vehicle other than a motorcar had been there. It had needed but little deduction to connect that with the contraband after he had found the cask in the upper room, but it had needed a more involved mental process to carry the discovery to the gipsy wagon. Furthermore, he was satisfied that the casks at which he looked were of the same seven he had already seen; that, in fact, it was this same wagon that had removed the contraband so mysteriously after his departure.

There at once leapt to his mind the thought that the persons who were responsible for their removal might have seen him poking about the place. If so, had they lain low until he was gone? And, by the same token, did they know he had found the body in the sand?

In that case, why had they left it untouched?

Was it because it had no connection with their smuggling activities, and they were only too glad to get the contraband away and break the last link with such a gruesome thing? Or had the gipsy been alone—had he come, as by some arrangement, to collect the brandy, and when he had done so departed, ignoring the other?

It might be so; yet, at the same time, Duncan was remembering that the contraband almost certainly had been brought in by some one who lived in the district; that such a line led straight to Little Soham, and that the same line fixed on the fisherman whom he had seen under several circumstances that must be called odd; there was the fleeting glimpse in Dr. Grunevald's private room, and the encounter just as he was driving into the inn-yard at Ockham. That was the occasion, too, when it might be said that there had also been great nearness—if not actual contact—between the fisherman and the gipsy tinker. Nor was he forgetting the matter of the broken tiller that had been used as a weapon in the murder.

He was not standing inactive while these thoughts passed through his mind. He had found what he had hoped and expected to find, and now was ready to put his theory to a further test. He had passed the curtain and was on his way to the door when a low, steady knocking on the floor of the caravan told him that Peter was making an urgent signal.

Duncan reached the door in one stride.

The moment he had opened it he knew why Peter had sent the urgent summons. Over the tops of the trees could be seen the glare of what he knew must be a moving car, and when he stood listening he could hear the low murmur of the engine.

He closed the door and relocked both locks. Then he leapt to the ground, where he found Peter standing on the alert. No words were necessary. Together they faded into the trees close at hand, and when they were in safe cover pulled up. If the car was only passing on its way north, then they were wise not to be seen to arouse comment. If, on the other hand, it should stop by the caravan—and Duncan was thinking of the possibility of some innkeeper picking up a keg of the contraband in this way—then they were free to observe without being seen.

A few moments later an indefinite glare gave way to a direct gleam from the headlamps, of the car as it swung into sight round the curve in the road.

Almost immediately it slowed down, and then, when it was almost opposite the Caravan, it drew into the side of the road and stopped. The engine was cut off and the driving lights turned out.

From their concealment, Duncan and Peter could see two figures emerge from the car and move across the lesser glow of the parking lights. They were so indistinct that they could not be certain of any detail, but they could see the two make straight for the rear steps of the caravan, and after a few moments disappear inside. It seemed that one must be the owner, for they could hear him speak roughly to the horse, and about his movements there was no attempt at concealment.

The watchers caught the gleam of a light through the door; then it slammed, and not a chink showed to reveal the presence of any one inside. It seemed evident that the pair within had not the slightest suspicion that their arrival had been observed.

After a few moments Duncan and Peter crept forward. They almost collided with the horse, which moved aside with a snort. They reached the side of the caravan, and with one accord crawled underneath, where, by crouching with uplifted heads, they could distinctly catch the sound of a voice that was declaiming above.

It was the last place just then in which Duncan expected to hear the tones of Dr. Harrison—Dr. Harrison, whom he had met in India and whom he believed to be still there; Dr. Harrison, who in India had slipped out of a very messy case and left his partner to bear the guilt alone; Dr. Harrison, whom jury and judge had complimented on his honesty in laying everything frankly before the police.

At first it was impossible to gather just what he was saying, for he seemed to be growling some indefinite complaint; and it was just as well, perhaps, for Duncan's mind was leaping from point to point in order to fit Harrison into the jumble of suspicions that were occupying his mind.

The fact that he had arrived here with one who, it seemed, was a gipsy tinker, pointed very strongly to the likelihood that they were mixed up in some illegal business together. But, whether it might be only in connection with the contraband traffic, or something else, was the question.

The fact that it was Harrison, however, was sufficient in itself to cause Duncan to give as close an ear as possible to what was being said above, and within the next few minutes he was to receive confirmation of more than one theory he had formed.

It was evident that something had angered Harrison considerably, for presently when Duncan and Peter could separate one word from another, they could gather that he was pouring his wrath upon the head of his companion.

"What beats me is why you didn't come to me before," he was saying savagely. "You knew yesterday what had happened there."

"Only in the afternoon," came the whining defence.

"The afternoon! Isn't that more than twenty-four hours? What have you been doing all that time?"

"I had to collect the stuff and make deliveries, hadn't I? After I saw Frost, I had to go back the whole way from Ockham and get it out before I was seen. How did I know I wasn't being watched?"

"Don't use that tone with me, or I'll wring your neck and pitch you under your own caravan! You take orders from me; and don't make excuses!"

The other whined submissively, and Duncan had little difficulty in picturing how quickly he would become subdued with Harrison threatening him. Harrison was not one to take back-chat from those who worked for him.

"You knew that this fellow who was snooping around had turned up something in the sand. You must have seen it when you picked up the kegs. Why didn't you bring it away as well?"

"It—it was too risky."

"Who the devil are you to talk about risk? For two pins I'd fix you so you wouldn't know the difference between a risk and a certainty. And let me tell you now that I'll do just that if you show any signs of gumming the works. It would have been easy enough for you to have picked that stiff out of the sand and bring it along, with the kegs. Then you could have dumped it where you dumped the other. I suppose you did dump the other where you said?"

"I did, mister, I did. It'll lie at the bottom of that pit until the crack of doom and no one will know."

"And that's where the other should be. If I'd known that snooper was going to appear on the scene—but it doesn't matter now. I'll deal with him. There are things on foot that are too important to be interfered with. That's why I wanted to see you to-night. I've got orders for you, and you see that they are obeyed to the letter, or it will be the worse for you."

"I'll do just as you say, mister, so long as you don't forget to pay me."

There was a slyness in the tone now that might have brought a fresh explosion from Harrison, but didn't. Indeed he laughed coarsely.

"Don't you worry, Lee, you'll get your share. How many more kegs have you to deliver?"

"Four."

"Well, you get along early in the morning and get rid of them. Then carry on with your usual work. You can keep about the district, for I may want you at any moment, but don't be seen in Little Soham or Ockham. If I want you, I'll send word by Frost."

"All right, mister."

"I suppose you have some of that stuff on tap?"

"I can manage a drop, mister."

Harrison laughed again, and there was the sound of footsteps as some one moved about. Then followed the clink of glasses, and a little later Harrison cleared his throat and swore affably.

"That's the best stuff I've struck for many a day. I wish now you had dropped one of these kegs with me."

"Have one out of the next lot, mister?"

"I would, only I'll be a long way from here by then. Give me another shot."

There was the clinking of glass again.

By the time Harrison was coming down the steps Duncan and Peter were back in the wood. They watched while he turned the car and drove off, and continued to wait until the gipsy re-entered the caravan and closed the door, but the moment it slammed, Duncan touched Peter's arm.

"Come on," he whispered, "that fellow will be safe until the morning. We've got to follow Harrison."

They crept out to the grass and, once away from the caravan, began to run. When they reached the motor-cycle it took only a moment for Peter to swing it round and put his foot on the starter. Duncan swung himself astride the pillion, and as soon as they were on the main road Peter sent the powerful machine along at a very different pace from that which had marked their outward journey.

They shot through Ockham like a streak; a lone constable gaped at the monster that was upon him and out of sight almost before he grasped what it was. He had never before known a motor-cycle travel with little more noise than a whisper.

Beyond Ockham Peter picked up the rear light of a car. It, too, was travelling at a good pace, but by the time the car reached the fork where one could turn off for Benham or continue towards Little Soham, he was close behind.

At a touch from his passenger, he eased his pace. The car kept straight on, but when it reached the second road. On the right, it turned. This was the same road by which Duncan had reached Dr. Grunevald's sanatorium from Little Soham.

Duncan was not surprised when Harrison turned his car into the gates of the sanatorium. The discovery that the man whom he believed to be a dangerous criminal was mixed up in some way with the matter upon which he was engaged, and the scraps of evidence he had obtained in the gipsy caravan, had given him much fresh food for thought, even though it had not helped clear up many questions.

Now, however, that he had seen with his own eyes this bold approach of Harrison's to the sanatorium, he considered it reasonable to regard Harrison as a fresh link in the chain.

For instance, there was a definite connection between Harrison and the gipsy whom he had called Lee; a possible connection between the gipsy and the fisherman from Little Soham, strengthened by what he had overheard in the caravan; between the gipsy and the Martello Tower, and—quite positive now—the tower and the murdered man whom he, Duncan, had found in the sand; between the fisherman and Dr. Grunevald; Grunevald and Harrison; Grunevald and the young Arab, Prince Faud, who in turn certainly pointed a connection with Sergeant Peel; and, hence, between Prince Faud and Peel jointly with Harrison.

But of what those various links might be composed, or how much tension they would stand, was a very different matter. And Duncan was remembering that, so far, he had failed utterly to make personal contact with Sergeant Peel. Peel might have discovered some of these things and be working quietly out of sight in search of some definite proof that would enable him to make an open charge.

There were many other details to be considered, such as the identity of the murdered man, and any possible connection between him and the sanatorium. If it should be found, as Duncan was beginning to suspect, that he might be Prince Faud's personal medical attendant, Dr. Raas, who had left so hurriedly and mysteriously, then a very important line might be opened up. Whatever that might be, he felt more strongly than ever: that there was something much more important and far deeper than ordinary smuggling activities beneath the mystery. He could not explain Harrison's being concerned only with such comparatively small business, for Harrison had been the chief medical officer in a big native state; and Dr. Grunevald's place in the affair was still unsettled. Was he mixed up in anything of a shady nature? It seemed incredible that a man of his standing should be, and yet Duncan was by no means easy in his mind about his brief visit to the specialist. There was the fact that the place was patronised by people of the greatest prominence and respectability, yet one could not ignore the equally strong fact that the determined attempt to murder him had come from an ambush within the grounds of the same estate.

Duncan did not attempt to prove these matters further just now. He wanted to put the second part of his theory to the test that night, for by this he knew he might be able to prove whether his reading of Peel's notes had been faulty or not.

Therefore, when they were some distance past the gate, he leant over Peter's shoulder.

"Turn and drive back towards Little Soham. There is a road there that turns off at a sharp tangent just before we get to the village. I want you to take that. I will tell you where to stop."

Peter nodded and skidded round in a dangerous circle. Then they flashed back past the gates of the sanatorium, and, turning to the right again, were once more on the road to Little Soham.

A moment more, and his lamp showed the angle that Duncan had mentioned. Peter shot into the branch on the left and almost immediately they began to mount a gradual slope.

It continued for half a mile or so, then they came out under a low ridge that ran at the back of Little Soham, from which in the daytime one could see across the marshland and saltings right along to the North Sea.

At another signal from Duncan Peter drew up. Duncan slid to the ground.

"Shut off the engine and turn off all the lamps. We may be here some time."

"What's the game?" asked Peter as he obeyed the instructions.

Duncan looked about him. The night had turned beautifully warm for so late in the year, and overhead the stars made a brilliant spangled carpet Of the heavens. There was no moon. It was a perfect night for many purposes, lawful and otherwise.

"Down there," Duncan told Peter, "is French Creek. And this is Thursday night."

"I've got it. You think something happened down there on a Thursday night that interested Peel, and he made a note of it."

"Just about that, Peter. I've got a theory I want to test, so let's find a dry spot and sit down. I want you to keep your ears open for any sound and your eyes peeled for any lights. If anything does come it should be from down the river towards the sea, if my theory is any good. In fact I shouldn't be surprised if we first noticed something well out to sea and coming landwards."

More than an hour passed without a single thing occurring to fulfil Duncan's prophecy. Now and then they caught the sound of a car somewhere inland, and once they saw some lights far out at sea. But that was all. They might have been alone in an almost empty world, so removed did they seem from all other human activity. Not a single light showed down in Little Soham. It might not even be in existence for all they could see.

But when another half-hour had been piled on to that hour, something did occur which caused Duncan to stiffen with keen interest. A light appeared suddenly out at sea, but much nearer than they had seen it before; and instead of a scarcely perceptible movement this was approaching the shore at a very fast speed. Then on the still night air there sounded a faint buzzing like that of an angry insect, a sound that grew in volume but not in tempo as the light drew nearer and nearer the shore. Then the light vanished in the direction of the point Duncan knew marked the entrance to the river which connected Little Soham with the sea. It was impossible yet to be certain that it had entered the river, but it did seem reasonable to connect the sound with the light, for when the light vanished behind the point, the buzzing rhythm grew perceptibly less.

Not for long, however. Within a few minutes the light came into view once more, this time actually in the river, and with this the sound again rose on the still air.

At no time did it become too insistent upon an inattentive ear. Indeed, had Duncan and Peter not been on the alert for something of the sort, they might easily have put it down to the passage of a car in the near distance, proof that the exhaust of a powerful engine was well muffled.

Straight up the river it came, and as it drew nearer and nearer to the entrance to French Creek Duncan watched it intently. There was not the slightest doubt in his mind now that they were watching the inward course, probably surreptitious, of a very fast and high-powered craft. Would it turn into French Creek? On that hung the whole fabric of his theory.

And it did. He relaxed involuntarily as the lights moved swiftly, to the left as they sat, and then seemed to take a way up through the marshes, twisting and winding so much at times that they lost sight of it. Then suddenly it vanished and did not reappear again.

"That's that, Peter. My theory seems to hold water so far. We'll finish the test and then push off. I think I shall be in a position by then to fit several pieces into a jigsaw.

"After a moderate space of time that boat should again be seen as it comes down French Creek, then, according to my theory, it should continue on up the river until it reaches Little Soham. We shall be there, Peter, to watch its arrival from the security of one of those old sheds by the jetty. I know one where we can wheel in the machine."

They got astride the motor-cycle, and within five minutes were slipping silently along the main street of Little Soham. The whole village was in darkness. They reached the shed by the jetty without meeting a soul, and there in the darkness, by the half-built boat, they pushed the machine

"I'll just have a look outside," Duncan murmured while Peter eased the motor-cycle back on its stand.

He slipped out into the passage and made his way to the jetty. From the side of this he could see the collection of boats riding at anchor at full tide.

Switching on his torch, he passed the beam over the collection and then, for a good ten seconds or so, he held the spot dead on one of the craft. Half a minute later he was back beside Peter.

"We'll get going," he told the lad.

"Is he coming up river now?"

"No. Somewhere or somehow my theory has come unstuck. The fast power-boat that I thought was the one we heard going up French Creek is out here and lying at her moorings, with her canvas cover made fast. There's a serious flaw somewhere, but we won't find it to-night in Little Soham, and it would be a fool's move to expect to find the explanation in French Creek now. We'll get back to Benham. We at least have something that should interest Inspector Clark."

They were about half a mile out of Little Soham on their way to Benham when the beams of Peter's headlight picked up a figure on the road. It was another motor-cyclist coming towards them, and during the brief moment that they had a clear view of the other, Duncan saw something that caused him to wonder if after all his theory was as faulty as it had seemed a few minutes before.

He was almost certain that the other motorcyclist was the Little Soham fisherman, Abel Frost.

CHAPTER EIGHT

DR. GRUNEVALD was in an uneven frame of mind. Things were by no means working out according to schedule. Indeed, that distinguished gentleman would have given a great deal at this moment if he had never been drawn into the affair that had developed so differently from what he had expected.

Had he but been the possessor of a large personal fortune there would have been no more horrorstricken person to be found than he when certain proposals had been made to him. Unfortunately, he was almost entirely dependent upon the fees he received from the distinguished and wealthy patients who from time to time became residents in his sanatorium, and the useful but dangerous income derived from certain unlawful activities, in which he took a passive rather than an active part

For, above all things, Dr. Grunevald was passionately engrossed in his private research work, the results of which were already proving of considerable value to humanity. It was, however, a most expensive work, and on many occasions Dr. Grunevald was at his wits' end to find the necessary money to meet urgent demands.

It was this same unlawful course on which he had allowed himself to wander in order to add to his about the same Arab youth? There had also been a man from Scotland Yard poking about for some days before that, but Harrison had told him that he had got rid of him. Just how, he did not say, but now, in view of other happenings, Dr. Grunevald was wondering how much meaning he could put into those words "got rid."

Then, to cap matters, there was the serious attempt at open murder that had been made upon Hugh Duncan.

In this his strong objections had been over-ruled, with no consideration at all for possible consequences.

Harrison had instructed him that all patients must be brought in from the grounds that afternoon, that all servants that he did not trust should also be kept indoors, and that his own two Yankee gunmen, who had arrived from Calcutta with him, should take control.

Harrison had pooh-poohed the idea of failure if it came to an attack upon Hugh Duncan. But he had been wrong. In spite of the hail of lead that had been poured into the car, Duncan had somehow got through unscathed, and it would be madness to suppose that he would suffer that murderous outrage without taking some form of action.

To put the thing briefly, Dr. Grunevald had been willing to indulge in unlawful activities so long as he felt that he ran little risk of discovery, but when he found himself implicated in such dangerous criminal operations as now revolved about him, he quaked in his cowardly heart.

But what could he do? He was asking himself this as he sat facing Dr. Harrison across the desk. To observe the pair at that moment it would have been difficult to believe that they were discussing multiple and major crime instead of the technicalities of some case under observation.

Harrison was perfectly well aware that the other was in the sort of funk that was likely to prove dangerous to his plans. If Grunevald broke now, then disaster would follow. But Harrison hadn't the faintest intention that he should break. He had handled more difficult cases than this.

"You're a fool," he told Grunevald bluntly, and in doing so was probably the only person to have addressed the distinguished scientist in such terms since student days. "You didn't expect to pull off a thing like this without possible hitches, did you?"

"I would never have gone into it had I known what it meant."

Harrison grinned and flicked the ash from his cigar. There was no funk bothering him. He was in a game that held more promise than any he had been in for a long time.

"Well, you're in now, and you'll stick. Besides, what are you afraid of? No one knows a thing, even if they do suspect."

"I'm worried about the man Duncan. I do not mind the police. They are easy enough to fool. But he is different. He claims to be an acquaintance of the Prince. Besides, I shall now have to go into Benham and identify the body they have found. That was a mistake."

"I grant you that. It wouldn't have happened if there had been more time, but we were pressed. But I've been thinking. Why need you identify it as Raas? Who's to know the difference if you say you have never seen the fellow before?"

"What if they demand that our Arab guest shall also view the body?"

"You can easily block that. You are his physician. All you have got to do is to say that he is in no fit state to undertake such a thing."

"I don't like—"

Harrison interrupted him swiftly.

"It isn't a case of what you like or don't like," he snarled. "I'm running this show, and you're doing what you are told. The sooner you understand that the better. If you feel that you'd like to pull out—why, go ahead, and then wait to see what the police will do when I tip them off about your other little activities."

"This—is blackmail!" gasped Grunevald.

"It's worse than that," snapped Harrison. "It's a straight threat, and, believe me, it's no empty one. Furthermore, if that isn't sufficient to keep you on the rails, I can soon find another means of taking care of you. Am I understood?"

"I understand that I have no choice, but at the same time you must listen to my advice. I think we are running too great a risk in doing as you suggest with Sir James Pinder. He is a man of such great prominence that there is a great danger."

Harrison leant forward.

"Will you get it into your head that no one is too important to deal with in this affair? We are after the answer to a certain question. Prince Faud knows part of that answer. Sir James Pinder knows the rest. One is no good without the other. Together they mean the biggest prize that has turned up in many a long day. This thing is big enough to tempt nations, let alone individuals. Therefore, whoever stands in my way has got to be thrust aside. Is that clear?"

"It won't do much good to handle Sir James Pinder as you have dealt with Dr. Raas."

"I have no intention of doing so. You may leave the details to me. What your attention must be given to is something different."

"And what is that?"

"Dealing with the man Duncan. I'll tell you now what I wouldn't tell you before for fear of your getting cold feet. I know him to be a private detective—often used by Scotland Yard."

"I see!" Grunevald was pale, but composed. "I see. Well? What am I to do? Surely you are not suggesting that I send and ask him to come here?"

"Do you take me for a fool?"

"Then what can I do?"

"He's going to come here, but not at our invitation. Some one else has attended to that for us. Look at this."

Harrison took from his pocket an envelope and tossed it across the desk. It was of the excellent quality provided by Dr. Grunevald for his patients if they cared to use it instead of their own, and it was unsealed. The scientist read the address that had been written in a fine, angular hand, and his brows rose, for what he saw was:

Hugh Duncan, Esq.,
Jermyn Street,
London, W.1.
Private and Urgent.

"What is this?" he demanded.

Harrison smiled.

"If you will read what it contains, you will find that it is an urgent appeal from Sir James Pinder to Duncan, asking him to come here at the earliest possible moment to rescue him. He adds that he believes that his life is in peril, and thinks that the life of another person whom Duncan is interested in is also in peril."

"Did Sir James Pinder actually write this?"

"He did."

"How did you get hold of it?

"Sir James paid his room attendant ten pounds to take that letter and see that it got into the post without going out in the house letter-box. Since the attendant knows what would happen to him if I ever caught him out, he was wise enough to bring the letter to me first. I steamed it open and found the contents decidedly interesting. Simple, wasn't it?"

"What are you going to do about it?"

"I am going to take another envelope and copy that writing—but it will not be the full address. That would entail delay. I have been able to learn where Duncan is staying. He is at Benham. He was a guest of the local police inspector, but is now at the inn. A young man, probably his assistant, is with him. If we can bag them both at the same time, so much the better, but, believe me, once we get the one into our hands, we shall not worry much about the other."

"But how will you get the letter to him?" Grunevald spoke collectedly; only his trembling hands betrayed his agitation.

"I shall manage that very easily. When he enters his room at the inn he will find this waiting for him. It will be somewhat soiled, as though it had been carried in the pocket of some one who found it in the road, for I shall convey the impression that Sir James Pinder threw it over the wall in the hope of it being picked up."

"It looks watertight," admitted Grunevald.

"It will be watertight when I have finished with it," grinned Harrison. "And when we get him here, that's where you come in. Then we will put the pressure on the other two—and they'll talk, Grunevald, they'll talk or—" and Harrison made a very sinister gesture with one hand.

The above conversation took place just before Harrison left to meet Lee, the gipsy, at Ockham, and before doing so he prepared another envelope as he had suggested (he was an expert forger—a fact that might have interested the admiring judge and jury years ago), then he despatched it to Benham by one of his men.

That is why when Hugh Duncan and Peter reached the inn about two o'clock in the morning after their checkmate at Little Soham, Duncan found an envelope lying on the floor of his bedroom, just as Harrison had prophesied.

Peter rode out of Benham the next morning alone. Duncan had decided to divide the work that was to be done, he himself handling the matters that had arisen out of the finding of the letter from Sir James Pinder, while Peter was to prosecute further inquiries into the mystery of the boat that had gone up French Creek the night before and had not come down again.

Peter's first objective was Little Soham. Bearing in mind Duncan's caution that he must watch his step, he thought it would be as well to try and locate this mysterious fisherman about whom his chief was suspicious before going on to French Creek.

The moment he rode on to the jetty he sensed that something had excited the unusually large number of men who idled and worked about the boats. Their customary taciturnity had given place to a low-voiced volubility as they stood in groups discussing some common subject.

But the moment Peter approached any group, the talking would cease and suspicious eyes would be turned upon him. Peter did not press his curiosity. He ascertained that the fisherman whose name Duncan had found to be Abel Frost was working alone over in his speed-boat, the only one, seemingly, who was unaffected by the general excitement. Yet, at the same time, Peter was sure that surreptitious glances were cast towards Frost by some of the others, and once he thought he detected one of them grin in a knowing way.

It was then he began to get a faint suspicion of what it might be, but he could not believe it possible, if he were right, that such news could have travelled so far by such an early hour.

Nevertheless, when he went along to the Jolly Sailor and asked for a cup of tea, he was able to overhear certain gossip that proved beyond doubt that he was right.

The cause of the excitement, it seemed, was nothing less than the news that Enoch Lee, the gipsy tinker who had been known to every man, woman and child in the district for twenty years or more, had been arrested by the police, and that in his caravan had been found several kegs of contraband spirits.

Peter was amazed. He knew that, shortly after their return to Benham the night before, Duncan had got hold of Inspector Clark and had told him what he would find if he gathered in the gipsy. He had also told him where Lee's caravan was standing. Duncan had strong personal reasons for wishing to have Lee arrested and kept out of contact with certain other persons for the time being, though he did not disclose these reasons to the inspector. It seemed, therefore, that Clark had acted with great promptitude, and that even for a country district the news had travelled like wildfire.

Peter wondered if Duncan would learn how it was so widely known. He knew that Duncan was on his way to Dr. Grunevald's establishment and felt that the same news might have some effect upon what Duncan might meet there. But he could not go to warn him now. He had his own job to do, and had been told to get it done as quickly as possible. Had he only done what he was half-tempted to do, and gone to the sanatorium, the whole course of his immediate future would have been different. But he decided reluctantly to stick to orders. So, when he had learned all that he could, he remounted his motor-cycle and rode back the way he had come until he reached the turning taken the night before. He swung into this and sent the machine up the grade at a rate that brought him to the ridge in a matter of moments.

Now, in the bright light of the sunny morning, he could see the whole panorama of the immediate district. At his feet was Little Soham, surrounded by its marshes, which in turn were separated from the saltings by a high dyke. Then the river that curved down inside the "island" with, on either side, the creeks that fed it from the marshes. Out at sea, visibility ceased abruptly where a low mist hung like a heavy cloud, but behind him he could see across the heath country almost as far as Dr. Grunevald's estate, while to the south he could see the stump that was the Martello Tower on Little Sahara. From a close study of the Government survey map, he knew which of the creeks beneath was French Creek, and he knew, too, that the road by which he had reached the ridge would take him along over the marshes close to the creek, for it continued on aimlessly for some distance before losing itself.

The idea of the procedure as suggested by Duncan was to get as far as possible on the motor-cycle and then go ahead on foot. He was in search of nothing more definite than any sort of craft that might fit in with the sort they had heard coming at great speed from the sea the night before, and whose light they had seen pass in

French Creek to vanish there, It didn't seem a difficult job to carry out, considering that, apart from this unknown craft, the only other one fitting the requirements was a speed-boat belonging to Abel Frost, and there was not the slightest doubt that when the mystery boat had come in from the sea the night before Frost's boat had been lying snug at her moorings at Little Soham.

He met not a soul on his way. Once he was out of sight of Little Soham he seemed to have the whole world to himself. He crossed several small bridges spanning ditches and small creeks, then he passed over a wider inlet, and, after another stretch of marshland, saw French Creek right ahead of him. It was by no means as attractive at such close quarters as it had been from the distance of the ridge with the sun shining upon it. But natural beauty had no part in Peter's thoughts just then. He was bound up in serious business, just how serious he was not to know until later.

He found a place where the marsh turf was banked up which would serve as a shield for the motorcycle, and when he had settled that he climbed the low bank and stood at the very edge of the creek, looking up and down.

Not much water was visible in either direction, for the course of the creek was very winding. But he could orient himself sufficiently by turning to look back at the ridge to estimate whether he was now above or below the spot beyond which he thought the mystery craft had proceeded the night before.

He concluded that he was higher up the stream, so turning his face towards the main river that passed Little Soham, he began to follow the course of the creek.

It was easy enough walking, though muddy, but the air was fresh and Peter was keen as mustard to discover the solution to the mystery of the night before.

The creek continued to wind as it neared the river, and from any given point he could see no more than a stretch of forty or fifty yards. It was for this reason that, when he did see a craft, it burst upon his vision so unexpectedly as to give him a mild shock. But a closer look soon showed him that it bore little likeness to what he had been expecting to find.

She was, in fact, only a ludicrous caricature of what he was looking for. She was, as far as could be seen, the hulk of a boat that must have been abandoned for years.

Her timbers were dirty and almost paintless.

What metalwork could be seen was black with rust.

Some rotten ropes hung over the side, and when Peter gave one a casual tug, it parted in his hand. So different was she from the polished speed-boat he was hoping to find that he laughed aloud.

"Well, I wonder what the chief would say if I showed him this old hulk," he mused. "She'd sink before she got to the river, let alone out to sea. Just the same, she must have been a pretty thing in her day. I'm no expert, but if those lines aren't jolly fine, then I've never sailed a boat."

And, indeed, any one who knew the subject would have agreed with him. Despite the rack and ruin, one could still detect the proud curve of the bows as they swept away into a perfectly proportioned body and then tapered beautifully to a yacht-like stern. She was, Peter judged, about forty feet long; but most of her top gear seemed to have been dismantled, and it was difficult to guess what she had been used for.

She lay so close to the bank that, becoming interested, he climbed on board. Here she revealed as much neglect as in her hull. Old rotten ropes littered the deck. The ironwork was rusty, the dirty deck was stained. Where a cabin-top had once been, the deck boards showed marks where it had been removed and the rough hatch-cover fitted. This, in turn—and to Peter, somewhat strangely was secured by a heavy canvas covering that looked strong and in much better condition than one would expect. And it was while he was looking down at this that Peter's eye lighted on something that caused his interest to quicken. It wasn't much. No more than a little pile of pipe-dottle which, seemingly, some one had knocked out on the hatch-cover. But what did strike Peter as remarkable about the tobacco was that it had the appearance of not having been there for any great length of time. He was remembering how hard it had rained the previous day. If that heap had been there then, it must have been soaked by the rain and scattered by the wind that had accompanied the storm.

He bent closer and examined it more carefully. Except for the natural moisture which becomes concentrated in the dottle at the bottom of the pipe, the heap looked to him as if it was exactly in the same condition as when it had been knocked from the bowl.

If that were so, then it could only have been deposited there since the storm the previous day. In that case, who had left it? And what had brought that person on board this old hulk? Peter was sufficiently intrigued to collect the heap and place it in an envelope; then he made his way along the deck until he could look down into the open cockpit, where the rusty remains of an engine could be seen.

This indeed revealed more signs of neglect than the hull or deck. As it appeared to Peter, it could not have propelled the boat a yard under its own power. It had apparently been left to the mercy of every storm and wind that blew.

Peter dropped into the cockpit and began poking around. The more he did so, the more evident was the ruin of a once fine engine. Then, because he was naturally thorough, he came upon a curious thing.

At one side was a wide mouthpipe covered with a screw-cap, which he took to be connected with the petrol tank. Unlike the rest of the metal work about him, this tap showed scarcely any signs of rust, and the short length of pipe which was visible was also free from the same blight.

Peter essayed to unscrew the cap and found that it worked quite easily. He removed it entirely and then his nostrils caught a strong whiff of petrol.

"Must have left some in when they deserted the boat," he murmured as he bent closer. It was then he made a second curious discovery. Not far down the pipe he could see liquid, and from the strength of the smell he knew it for good petrol.

He straightened up for a moment and made a quick calculation. He came to the conclusion that in a boat of this size the tank capacity could be considerable. He guessed a minimum of not less than fifty gallons. If that were so, then why had a full tank been left when the boat was abandoned?

He gazed about him thoughtfully. Then he replaced the cap and began an even closer investigation. Ten minutes later a startling thing happened. He was hanging on to a pleat on one side of the cockpit lining when he slipped to one side, and in so doing must have released an unseen catch, for, without warning, the whole side came away in his grasp.

Peter staggered against the engine, recovered himself, and then stood gazing in open-mouthed astonishment at what was now revealed through the opening.

He found himself looking into an inner cockpit that had been concealed by the false lining. And in that was one of the most powerful engines he had ever seen fitted to a boat of this size. Her cylinders and rod were wiped with meticulous care. Her bright parts were polished until even in the semi-gloom they winked at him.

Peter dived through the opening to get a better look at this strange discovery. He knew a good deal about engines, and it did not take him long to realise that he was looking at a most expensive one, and one, moreover, that was in regular and frequent use. The hand that had gone over it with loving care had not been absent long.

The magnitude of the discovery was only beginning to dawn upon him. So amazed was he at such an unexpected find on board this old hulk that the indications had not penetrated his mind. But now they began to do so, and he was not long in realising that his find, strange though it might be, was the very thing that Duncan had sent him out to seek.

His gaze now noted a narrow opening in the bulkhead where the driving-shaft passed from the engine to the sternpost. He moved towards it, his nostrils twitching as he did so under the assault of an odour that grew stronger with each step.

He found that he could just manage to squeeze through the opening into the dark hold that lay beyond, and now, so insistent did the odour become, he knew it must have its origin somewhere beyond the bulkhead. Peter was no pub-crawler, but he knew quite enough about spirits to identify this as the emanation of strong spirits, probably brandy.

He got out his pocket torch and flashed a beam into the darkness beyond. It revealed even more than he expected to find, for there, piled in four rows, were several kegs of what he guessed to be the same sort of contraband brandy that Duncan had found in the upper room of the Martello Tower.

His pulses raced. Here was something that would please Duncan no end. It would prove, too, that his theory had not been faulty at all. The events of the night had worked out exactly as he had anticipated, with the exception that there were two speed-boats instead of one, and this was this one camouflaged as an old hulk that had put them astray for the moment.

Highly elated, Peter turned back. All he wanted now was to get back to his motor-cycle and to reach Duncan as fast as it could take him. He wanted to see Duncan's face when he told him to what the dottle had led him. That was detective work after his chief's own heart.

But while he was carefully passing the engine a shadow filled the opening through which he had come.

He had a brief glimpse of a human figure bent down peering in at him. Realising his danger he sprang forward, ready to grapple with the other. But he reached the end of the compartment only in time to hurl his weight against the side of the outer cockpit that had been slammed into place.

And, as he recoiled, he heard a stream of low, quiet curses that were far more sinister than any amount of noisy threats.

CHAPTER NINE

WHEN he had seen Peter off on his mission to French Creek, Duncan did not leave the inn at once on his proposed visit to Dr. Grunevald's establishment.

He was not at all satisfied about the letter that he had received from Sir James Pinder, although after several analyses he had come to the conclusion that if it weren't genuine, it had been written by some one who, apart from being an exceptionally clever forger, possessed a remarkable insight into Sir James's character. For Duncan knew the noted archaeologist quite well, and could gauge fairly well what sort of letter he would write under duress.

One thing alone was sufficient to rouse Duncan's suspicions. This was the manner in which the letter had been delivered. Some one had placed or thrown it on the carpet of his bedroom, and an inquiry of the innkeeper had brought a denial that he knew anything at all about the letter, or that he or any servant of his had thrown a letter into the room in such a fashion.

It would have been a perfectly simple matter, Duncan saw, for some one to approach the inn through the garden at the back, open the window, and toss the letter in without being seen, since he and Peter occupied a somewhat isolated wing on the ground floor overlooking the garden.

Now, though, Sir James Pinder knew that Duncan was in the district, and knew that he was interested in the welfare of Prince Faud, Duncan had made no mention at all of where he was staying, and even if he had, he was at that time still the guest of Inspector Clark. Therefore it was, to Duncan's mind, quite impossible that Sir James could have directed any one to bring the letter to the inn at Benham.

But if he were right, then it seemed reasonable to suppose that the person who had ensured the delivery of the letter was anxious for his presence at Dr. Grunevald's.

In that case, who was so anxious to see him? Dr. Grunevald? Duncan was not prepared to answer that yet. Harrison? If Harrison were a factor in this multiple mystery into which he had plunged, then, from what he already knew and suspected of that gentleman, it was quite on the cards that he had a strong reason for getting Duncan inside the place. One thing was certain. Sir James Pinder would be no willing partner to any nefarious business; and yet Duncan would have been better pleased could he have defined the meaning of that expression that had flashed into Sir James's eyes when he mentioned that he was interested in Prince Faud.

"Well," he told himself as he stuffed his pipe, "it seems that some one desires my presence at Dr. Grunevald's sanatorium, so far be it from me to disappoint them. I'll go along and see what happens. It will at least be a means of making direct contact again with the interior of that eminently respectable establishment, and that is a thing I am very keen to do."

It was at this point that a knock came on the door of the sitting-room. The round, red face of the innkeeper came round the opened edge.

"There's some one to see you, sir."

Duncan's mind went at once to Inspector Clark, but when he asked if it were he, the innkeeper shook his head in quite a shocked way.

"It's no one from the local police station, sir. He's a queer-looking foreign fellow." The last with infinite condescension.

Duncan was instantly on the alert. It began to seem as if his name and whereabouts were known to several persons.

"I'll see him in here," he said promptly.

The landlord vanished. When he had gone Duncan slipped a small automatic into the side pocket of his jacket, and took up his place in front of the cosy wood fire that took off the chill of the morning.

The moment the door opened to admit the visitor he recognised the same dark-skinned fellow whom he had seen crouched so miserably over the fire at the inn at Ockham. Seen standing, the man showed a slender sinewy figure that suggested great strength. He salaamed respectfully.

"How—do you—be?" he said in laboured, stilted English.

"Peace be with thee," responded Duncan in Arabic.

The other had straightened up, and now an expression of surprised joy came into his dark eyes as he heard his own tongue spoken. So obvious was it that Duncan reproached himself for not having given him a word at Ockham. Whether he came as a friend or foe didn't matter to Duncan.

"Allah be praised," the man cried in Arabic. "Allah has indeed guided me." He changed as he spoke from unhappy misery into something hard and confident. He was no longer speechless among foreigners.

"What is thy name?" Duncan continued in the same tongue.

"Hussein ben Mustapha, ben Ismail, ben Hassan, ben—"

"Why have you come to me?" Duncan interrupted hurriedly.

Before the other could answer there was another knock at the door. This time the visitor proved to be Inspector Clark. He greeted Duncan, then gave him a knowing look and indicated the Arab.

"So he did come to see you, after all. I thought he was bluffing."

"I'm afraid you will have to explain, Clark. There seems to be something about this that I don't understand."

"Hasn't he told you, then?"

"He has had no time to do so. I have just asked him what brought him to see me."

"Well, I'll tell you all I know about it. But first I want you to know that we've gathered in that gipsy tinker Lee, and it was just as you said. We found four kegs of contraband brandy, and before we finish we'll find the other three that were in the Martello Tower."

Duncan thought of the innkeeper at Ockham, but said nothing. The man had trusted him as a sportsman, and he would be no stool-pigeon. Besides, he himself had consumed some of the stuff, and, to make matters worse, had enjoyed it immensely.

"I wish you'd tell me how you knew that we'd find that Lee had some of the contraband in his caravan," Clark went on. "That fellow has been around this district for twenty years or more, and I've never heard a whisper of anything against him other than that he does a little moneylending on the quiet."

"He ought to be in a position to do so if he has been raking in a profit off the other," was Duncan's dry and non-committal reply. "Now, about this fellow here—you seem to know something about his coming to me."

The Arab was watching Duncan intently, but he said nothing. When the inspector made reply he turned his head to watch him as closely. It was as if, knowing only a little English, he was trying to make his eyes help his ears.

Clark shrugged.

"It isn't much I know. He came into the police station about twenty minutes ago and asked for you by name. He couldn't pronounce it very well, but wrote it on a piece of paper. I asked him why he wanted you but he wouldn't say. You can guess that I was curious about him, for he is a good deal like the one who was murdered on Little Sahara."

Duncan's smile was sardonic.

"True. One was a Hindu from India, and this fellow is of Bedouin stock from Arabia. What next?"

"As I was reading your name, a constable came in to report that the gipsy caravan was coming along, so I told this fellow that he would find you at the inn. I instructed Constable Judd to see him along and to keep an eye on him until I could follow. That's all. May I listen while you ask him what he wants? I've got a hunch he may be able to tell us the identity of the dead man, and I want to know, too, what he is doing in this part of the country. It's my opinion that he may have had something to do with that affair."

"I haven't the slightest objection to your listening, my dear fellow, but I am doubtful if he knows English sufficiently to carry on in that tongue. It may be necessary for me to talk with him in his own language."

"Then you could tell me afterwards what he says."

"I could do that," admitted Duncan with an inward smile.

Then he turned to the stranger.

"Shall we speak in Arabic or English?"

"May it please thee to converse in my own tongue."

"Be it so. Tell me thy tale."

"There is little to say. Thanks be to Allah, I have found thee. Had I known it was thee whom I saw at the caravanserai in the other city I would have spoken then. I have come to thee because it is known to me that thou hast some interest in the young sheik's son of my country who sojourns in this land at present."

"Prince Faud?"

"It is he, effendi."

"What interest have you in him?"

"I have the honour to be in the confidence of His Highness the Sheik El Bakr, Sheik of El Wejh. I was entrusted secretly with the duty of watching over his son."

Had the words not verged on tragedy Duncan would have smiled at this naïve admission. It revealed how very simple and terribly remote from the complicated life of the West even the ruling caste of an Arab country could be. It certainly seemed ludicrous to regard this shivering and unhappy specimen as a secret bodyguard to protect a distinguished charge. Duncan reflected now that it was probably because some realisation of this had come to Sheik El Bakr that he had made request direct to the British Foreign Office to keep an eye on his son.

"Does Prince Faud know that you are here?"

"No, effendi. My presence was known to his *hakim*, Dr. Raas. It was his duty to give me word each day as to the welfare of His Excellency the Prince. For this purpose we would meet in a deserted fortress that stands in country similar to my own desert land."

Duncan knew that he must be referring to the Martello Tower on Little Sahara, and now his interest was keen enough.

"Three—four days ago I went there as usual to meet him," the other went on. "But it was impossible to approach. I saw strange men there. They were coming in and out, and I was afraid to draw near. I withdrew, thinking that Dr. Raas would also refrain from going to the place that day. I returned on the following day and found the place empty. I waited for some hours, but Dr. Raas did not come. I have visited the fortress at the same hour each day, but still have I seen nothing of Dr. Raas. I did not dare go to the large house where His Excellency is staying. My instructions forbade me that. But I was greatly troubled for I had lost touch completely. In my dilemma I wrote to an effendi in London who is a friend of Sheik El Bakr. He is to be found in the great building where the foreign affairs of this country are conducted. This morning I had a communication from another place, the headquarters of the police of this land."

"You mean a place called New Scotland Yard?"

"That is the name, effendi."

Duncan frowned. What the devil was the Yard doing in writing to this fellow and giving him his name and address without informing him that they had done so. But he only told the other to go on.

"So, effendi, since that address was the building of the police in this city I came from Ockham to find thee. The effendi's name is not unknown to me. There was the matter of one Beni Said from El Wejh in Cairo which the effendi will no doubt recall."

Duncan remembered the case well enough. But just now his mind was occupied with the unusual behaviour of the Yard. He turned to Clark.

"Have you received any letters for me this morning?"

The inspector's mouth opened and shut with a snap.

"What a stupid thing. I'm terribly sorry, Mr. Duncan. There is a letter for you on my desk. I was expecting you to come in, and I never thought about it when I came along after this fellow. It came in this morning's post. I'll get it at once."

With that he vanished, and Duncan turned back to the Arab. If, as he now suspected more strongly than ever, the murdered man had been Dr. Raas, then it was obvious that this man must view the remains and identify them if possible.

He spoke quietly, but at some length. He had no more than finished when the inspector returned with the letter. Duncan tore it open and saw that it was from Chief-Inspector Pointer. It enlightened him to a certain extent regarding his strange visitor.

DEAR DUNCAN (the letter ran)—I am enclosing the translation of a letter in Arabic which Morley of the F.O. received yesterday. The translation is Morley's. Return it to the Papers Dept. The writer seems to be in a very disturbed state of mind regarding something or other connected with Dr. Grunevald's sanatorium and the young Arab, Prince Faud. He is too vague to be coherent, and we don't know what is behind it. We are replying to him—in English—giving him your address as care of the police station, Benham. We think it best that you should see him and find out what it is all about. If he has anything definite to tell, you may, if you like, send him up to London, and we'll do the rest. I leave it to your discretion. Still no news from Peel. I am getting seriously concerned about him, but I know you will inform us the first moment you hear anything. He may be on something important which prevents him sending in any reports. But I doubt this,—Yours,

(Signed) ALFRED POINTER.

Duncan quickly scanned the translation that was enclosed. It was a very incoherent version of what his visitor had just told him. He had already made up his mind that the fellow was perfectly genuine, and he was hoping that he might find him useful. For this reason he knew he must handle him carefully. He felt compassion for the poor wretch who had come all alone to this strange country of the West on a duty that was almost impossible to perform. Anything less like a highly-placed Secret Service man it was difficult to imagine.

"This man is not employed in any criminal activities," he told the inspector quietly. "I am ready to vouch for him personally. He has told me his story and why he desired to see me. He was authorised by Scotland Yard to come to me. It is possible, however, that he may be of some assistance in identifying the body of the man I found on Little Sahara,"

"Will you come along now, then? The corpse is in the back room at Tom Hatt's. He acts as the local undertaker."

Duncan agreed, and spoke in Arabic to the stranger.

"We believe that Dr. Raas may have met his death," he told the Arab. "I want you to come along and see if it is

he. You must show no anger. There must be no revenge—
by you. That is for the police. I will look after you, and
later we can go into matters."

"May Allah bless the effendi," said the Arab gruffly,
his dark eyes flashing.

It was only a few minutes' walk to Tom Hatts place,
where he carried on a variety of activities, including a
garage and hiring business, carpentry, undertaking and
even hairdressing.

On the way they had to pass the police station. It was
while they were doing so that the Arab, who was walking
between Duncan and the inspector, caught the former's
arm and pointed. Then he spoke rapidly in Arabic.

What he said was:

"Effendi, I have seen that cart at the fortress of which
I told you."

He was pointing at the red and yellow-painted
caravan that had been brought in with Lee, the gipsy.

But all Duncan told the inspector was:

"He says he has seen that caravan before."

Inwardly, however, Duncan was keenly interested, for
in this odd way he had received what he had been
searching for—confirmation of his certainty that the
caravan had been at the Martello Tower. He was
impatient to get back to the inn, for now he was ready to
put to the test one of the most startling theories that he
had yet formed.

The identification was a matter of moments only. As
soon as he laid eyes on the dark features of the murdered
man, the Arab turned to Duncan.

"It is the *hakim*," he said simply.

Duncan translated to Clark, then he caught the
Arab's arm.

"No revenge! This is more than a tribal matter. This
must be left to the Government."

He turned to Clark again as, the Arab stalked
gloomily out of the building. "I've got to get back to the
inn at once, and I want you to come with me."

"What is it—something about this?"
"Limekilns," was Duncan's laconic answer.

CHAPTER TEN

INSPECTOR CLARK'S curiosity was only slightly appeased when, in his sitting-room at the inn, Duncan displayed his Government survey map of the district. During the past few hours he had studied that map again and again. It was what he had overheard while lying beneath Lee's caravan the night before, which had inspired this interest.

"Look here, Clark."

The inspector bent over the table and saw that the point of Duncan's pencil was resting on a green patch that lay about midway between the towns of Ockham and Loxley.

"This is marked as the 'Old Limekilns.' By the scale of the map you can see that the spot is about four miles from Ockham, and the same from Loxley. Do you know it at all?"

"I've been over the place once or twice; not more. It's all covered with scrub growth and very wild."

"But it must have been resorted to at some time or other. If not, what is the meaning of 'Old Limekilns'?"

"Oh, that is right enough. Away back in the middle of last century they burnt lime there. They got it from close at hand. But the place was abandoned years ago."

"I see, it's now a sort of no man's land."

"That's it."

"Do you know how many kilns there are?"

"Not exactly, but only a few—say four or five."

"I see a line marking a road or track here on the map. Can we reach the place that way?"

"I should think it would be pretty rough and overgrown, but we might manage it. Why on earth do you want to go there?"

"I'd rather not say just now, but I wish you would make arrangements for a couple of men to come along with us. We shall want some tackle too. I would suggest block and rope and some timbers to which we can hang the tackle."

"You mean—over those pits?"

"Exactly."

"But what for?"

"To see what we can find. I've got a theory. That is all I can say now. Will you arrange this? If you'd rather not, I can manage it some other way."

"Oh, I'll fix it. Tom Hatt has plenty of tackle. When do you want to go?"

"As soon as possible."

And although he looked at Duncan as if he thought he must be crazy, the inspector went off to make the necessary arrangements.

He had not exaggerated the difficulty of the way. From a mile or so near Ockham a poor road led along to a small and remote village. From here the road rapidly degenerated into no more than an indeterminate way that grew steadily worse as they proceeded, Duncan and Inspector Clark in the latter's sturdy little two-seater, Tom Hatt's ancient lorry bumping along behind. Duncan had left the Arab at the inn in Benham to await his return.

Bit by bit Clark began to recall the place as he had seen it years ago, but it had suffered a great change since then, and when they did finally come to the area in which the abandoned pits lay, it was almost impossible to see them, so overgrown was the ground with bushes.

Indeed, they were forced to get out of the car and proceed on foot, but while they were still stumbling about, Tom Hatt had found a way through the bushes.

"I used to come out here when I was a boy," he told them. "This was an open path then. But if I remember aright, it ought to take us right in to the top of the pits."

They followed him. The way, mounted steeply up, and as they came into a somewhat open space Duncan could see beneath and to the left the openings at the bottom of the kiln where the fire would have been.

It was a picture of ruin and desolation. The bottom was blocked with tumbled heaps of stone, and the whole was tangled up with bushes and weeds. In the very centre a small tree was growing. In a few more years the place would be entirely buried from view.

Strangely enough, however, the path they were following grew more easy to negotiate as they proceeded. Then it came out on to a flat, grassy platform where there were visible the open mouths of five primitive kilns.

It is not quite correct to say the mouths of all the kilns were open. Three gave free enough entry to anything that might fall or be thrown in from the top, but the other two were choked with baulks of old, rotting timbers on which had collected a heap of wind-drift rubbish.

Duncan drew up and studied them one by one. Inspector Clark and Tom Hatt watched him curiously. Neither of them had the faintest idea what they were doing at this outlandish spot.

Suddenly Duncan turned and looked at Hatt, a big round-faced man with shrewd blue eyes.

"Tell me, Hatt," he said casually, "suppose you wished to dispose of something that you didn't want any one to find for a long, long time—something that it wasn't easy to get rid of through the usual channels—and you knew of this place, into which of these pits would you drop it?"

Hatt looked back at Duncan as if he thought the London man was a bit scatty, but since he was, apparently, a friend of Inspector Clark's—and he was doing pretty well out of the police just now—he would try to humour him.

"Well, sir," he drawled at last, "if I wanted to get rid of, say, some stolen goods and knew about these pits—and you couldn't find a better place, sir —I'd pick one of those two on the far side."

The two that he indicated were partially blocked with timber baulks and rubbish.

Duncan now looked at Clark.

"And you, Inspector?"

"It would all depend on whether I was in a hurry or, not. If I had little time, I'd drop the sack into the first hole I came to. If I wasn't pressed, I think I'd do what Hatt says."

"And so would I," agreed Duncan.

He gazed at the two holes.

"And," he went on presently, "of those two, I think I'd pick the one that is almost completely blocked. There is an opening there through which a good-sized bundle might be dropped, and while being the least likely to attract the curious, it must be so dark inside that even if one lay quite close to the edge, I doubt if it would be possible, to see any detail. At any rate I'm going to have a try, and I'll use my pocket torch."

He suited the action to the word, and while the others watched he made his way across the grass until he was close to the top of the pit indicated.

He knelt down, then lay flat. Taking out his pocket torch, he switched it on and directed the beam through the opening, which was no more than three feet long by a foot and a half wide.

The light stabbed through the mephitic gloom until it reached the bottom some forty feet below. But here was such a conglomeration of leaves and other rubbish that Duncan could not pick out one detail from another. He tried again at the next pit with a like negative result.

To inspect the remaining three was a simple matter. When he had finished his two companions looked at him inquiringly. It was plain that the inspector was beginning to get somewhat impatient.

"I wish you would return to your lorry and get your son to help you bring up the tackle," Duncan said to Hatt. "I want to fix it so that I can be lowered into the first pit, and possibly the second. Please be as quick as you can."

Hatt took himself off, though it was quite plain that he didn't have much faith in Duncan's sobriety. When he was gone, Duncan interrupted the inspector in something he started to say.

"I think the moment has come when I should explain why I asked you to have Hatt come here," he said quietly. "You seem to be under, the impression that I am following some wild fancy. For many reasons I hope devoutly that you are right. On the other hand, I have formed a theory that there is still another body to be uncovered in this district, and a certain process of reasoning leads me to think that it may be found in one of these pits. We shall see presently, whether I am right, or wrong."

So dumbfounded was the inspector that speech was beyond him. He walked instead to the nearest pit, where he stood peering down until Tom Hatt and his son arrived lugging the tackle.

It did not take long for the four men to erect the baulks in tripod form over the pit selected. When that was done the block and tackle were bent on, and when a foot-loop had been fixed, Duncan prepared to go down.

During the erection of the timber it had been necessary to clear away most of the rotten baulks that almost covered the opening, so that now Duncan had clear swinging space for his descent.

Clark had worked in silence, but just before Duncan was ready to go down he stepped forward.

"I'll go down," he said curtly. "If there is down there what you think, then it is a matter for the police of the district. It looks a dirty hole, and anyway it's my job."

But Duncan shook his head.

"This is my pigeon, Clark, and I'll pluck it. Stand by, Hatt."

Before the inspector could say more, Duncan caught the rope, and Hatt braced against it ready for the tension. His son joined him, and then, at a sign from Duncan, they began to lower him into the pit.

Clark was right about the place being a dirty hole. The air was sour with the smell of decomposing rubbish. It grew more and more foul as Duncan descended, but he gave no sign beyond an offended twitching of his nostrils.

When he was within a few feet of the bottom, or, rather, of the heap of matter that lay on the bottom, he saw something that made the atmosphere a matter of no moment.

At one side, amongst some rotting leaves and what he had taken from the top to be part of that mass of decaying vegetation, was something of greenish hue which was revealed now as being of a very different nature.

It looked to him, from where he swung, like the sleeve of a khaki shirt. Then he saw a human hand attached to the sleeve, but whether the latter contained an arm that was attached to a body was not evident until Duncan had shouted instructions for the two above to lower very slowly, and then, when he could reach out and scrape away some of the unpleasant mess of leaves, he found a terrible thing.

The body of a man was revealed. It lay face upwards. It was garbed startlingly in hiker's kit—khaki shirt and shorts, golf stockings and heavy walking-boots. A walker's thumb-stick was lying among the leaves not far away, and still clinging to the scalp over one ear was a jaunty green beret.

Duncan moved the head ever so little to get a better view of something that he had glimpsed beneath the green beret. Now he could see sufficient to tell him how the unfortunate fellow had met his death. The side of the skull had been smashed in by a terribly savage blow.

A dozen questions surged through Duncan's mind, but these faded before the amazing and shocking fact that this body which he had found in the bottom of a noisome pit was all that remained of Detective-Sergeant Peel.

CHAPTER ELEVEN

THE finding of Detective-Sergeant Peel's body in such circumstances was no little shock to Duncan, and he knew that it would cause both puzzlement and anger at Scotland Yard. The dead man's superiors there would find it difficult to understand why Peel, engaged upon what had seemed a matter of no more than ordinary routine, should have met such a fate.

Duncan was not as surprised as he might have been had he not found Peel's private note-book in the upper room of the Martello Tower. From the very beginning those last three pages of cryptic entries had quickened his interest, and he had deciphered them with what he knew now to be a certain accuracy; but they had given no hint at all that Peel had stumbled on to something as important and as sinister as this brutal murder seemed to indicate.

Duncan knew, of course, that the inquiry would now come under the direct authority of the Suffolk police, but knowing as he did how chary those at the Yard were of stepping on the toes of local people, Duncan thought it quite possible that he would be asked to continue to represent the central headquarters. Certainly nothing could make him keener than he now was to solve the mystery. He had been growing more and more absorbed in the problem ever since he set out to cross Little Sahara on foot.

So when he had imparted the startling information to Inspector Clark, and later at Benham had discovered, after a telephone message had been put through to Scotland Yard, that it was to be as he had thought, he left the local inspector to take things up with his superiors, and returned to the inn to tackle his own phase of the matter.

It was now about three in the afternoon. He had said nothing at all to Clark about his faint distrust of Dr. Grunevald's sanatorium.

In the first place, he knew he would have to have something very definite to put forward before the local authorities would credit any tale of nefarious doings against that eminently respectable establishment.

Duncan himself was none too definite in his own mind about it. His solitary visit had been too brief to learn much. Dr. Grunevald had been a pattern of all that one in his position should be.

True, there had been that fleeting glimpse of the fisherman from Little Soham who had roused his interest on several occasions, but that did not give him a reason for suspecting Dr. Grunevald—of what? He could not say himself.

But his absolute certainty that Dr. Harrison had been implicated at least once in a crime, the presence of Prince Faud in the home, the undoubted murder of his personal medical attendant, Dr. Raas, and the rather puzzling attitude of Sir James Pinder, were all factors which Duncan believed to be interrelated, and among them, he felt certain, lay the solution to the several mysteries that he had come up against.

Contraband was serious in itself, worse when linked with murder, but Duncan felt even this was not all that bound such oddly assorted persons together. He was beginning to feel more and more that Detective-Sergeant Peel had stumbled upon something of the mystery during the ordinary course of his duty, and that in order to close his mouth he had been murdered out of hand. He believed, further, that Dr. Raas had also been eliminated for some similar reason; and heaven knew there had been as cold-blooded an attempt to assassinate himself as one could conceive.

Which brought to his mind the thought of Peter. He began to feel a little uneasy about the lad. While his errand to French Creek was one in which he would probably require to use both discretion and time in unlimited quantities, it did not seem to Duncan that he should have needed the better part of the day for the job.

It might seem foolish to be anxious for the lad during the broad light of a sunny day, but Duncan remembered the murderous attack that had been staged upon himself, no less recently than the previous afternoon.

So engrossed was he with his own thoughts that he had almost forgotten the minor problem of Hussein, the Arab, until he entered his sitting-room at the inn and found him still there.

He knew now that the other was deeply worried at his inability to make direct contact with Prince Faud and thus hear from his own lips that he was all right, and he had already learned how the fate of Dr. Raas had filled him with misgivings. Duncan remembered that he was, without doubt, high in the confidence of the Sheik El Bakr, and as that shrewd ruler was not one to suffer fools gladly, he thought it very probable that his representative, odd fish though he might appear, was no little factor in his own surroundings. Here, however, everything was completely alien to him, and Duncan's natural kindness made him want to do something to help the other. He was startled and amused when he learned the most immediate cause of the other's unhappiness.

"It is the food in this land, effendi" he said, after, some urging. "At the great caravanseraies in London it was possible to procure some of the simple foods of my country, but here it is impossible to find among the bazaars or caravanseraies what I seek."

Duncan's voice was gravely concerned when he replied.

"These small cities are remote from the bazaars, even as the scattered oases of the desert. Nor does the date palm grow in this land. The sweetmeats, too, are different

from the delectable cakes of Arabia. Nevertheless, it may
be in my power to make some arrangements for you. I
shall see what can be done."

"But the coffee, effendi. It is worse than the water of
the sour wells."

"That, too, shall receive my care," promised Duncan.

"May Allah guard thee, effendi, and fill thy house
with many children and grandchildren. The gratitude of
Hussein ben Mustapha will endure while he sojourns in
this life."

"It can be expressed in a material form."

"Effendi, I am thy servant as Allah is my witness."

"Then I have words for your ear. We shall speak with
guarded tongues, for none must know."

"The desert itself harbours many secrets, effendi."

"There is a desert nearer here whose secret I would
learn," rejoined Duncan quickly. He sat down close to the
Arab and disclosed what was in his mind. Few persons in
England could have understood what was being said even
had they been able to overhear, for Duncan was using the
little-known Arabic of Central Arabia, the same medium
which Sir James Pinder had used in conversing with
Prince Faud.

From time to time Hussein would make a gesture of
assent, or murmur some elaboration of phrase that
Duncan had used, but for the most part he listened in
silence, his dark eyes fixed gravely upon Duncan. And
they were now piercing, brilliant, hard—the eyes of a
desert hawk, true Arab eyes.

When the palaver was over, Duncan went along to the
kitchen of the inn, and after a talk with the landlord set
about preparing a pot of coffee such as had never been
brewed in that inn kitchen in all its two hundred years'
existence.

It was by no means the thick, syrupy concoction for
which the soul of Hussein craved, but it was the nearest
thing possible to provide at the moment, and rarely had
Duncan been embarrassed with such expression of

gratitude as when Hussein saw the heavy black liquid sticking to his spoon.

Following that, Duncan had a second interview with the landlord. It was very brief, for his instructions were few.

"I shall be remaining in my room," he told the other. "I have some particularly urgent work to get through, and do not wish to be disturbed under any conditions; not even by Inspector Clark if he comes along. You will see to this?"

"No one shall get into that part of the inn, sir. You can leave it to me. You will ring when you want something? And the foreign gentleman, sir?"

"He will be leaving soon."

With that Duncan returned to his rooms. Half an hour later, when the figure of an Arab might have been seen passing out of Benham at dusk, the key of Duncan's room was turned on the inside, and the landlord was watching that no one approached the door.

It was dark when the same Arab figure could have been seen approaching the door of Dr. Grunevald's private sanatorium.

Dr. Grunevald and Dr. Harrison were together in the former's comfortable room when a maid tapped at the door to announce the caller. She held out a small tray on which reposed a card. Dr. Grunevald picked it up, and after a frowning glance, passed it to Harrison.

It was a much larger piece of pasteboard than would have been used by an Englishman. It bore some Arabic letters in the centre, and pencilled in awkward English beneath was:

"To ask the doctor effendi for welfare seeming of Excellency Prince Faud."

"This is the fellow we've heard about," said Harrison in quick low tones. "You'd better leave him to me."

Grunevald did not look at all satisfied, but the presence of the maid stilled any protest he might have made. He hadn't the faintest idea that this same maid was, in reality, Mary Trent, a lady who for some time past had become a partner in the adventures of Dr. Harrison.

"As you will," he muttered. "But you will be careful?"

"You can safely leave things to me," smiled Harrison. "I think the best place to see him is here."

"Then I shall leave you. In any event, I have a patient to see."

With that Grunevald rose and passed out by the same door through which Hugh Duncan had seen the fisherman from Little Soham vanish. When he was gone Harrison looked at the trim maid.

"Grunevald is getting cold feet," he said carelessly. "He'd have complete paralysis if he knew everything."

"Who is this fellow at the door?" she asked quickly.

"Some bird who has been hanging about ever since we have been here. He met Raas once or twice. I'll deal with him so he won't worry us again."

"Be careful. Things are going on outside."

"What do you mean?"

"I've been trying to get a private word with you for more than an hour. The police found a body to-day."

"The devil they did! Where?"

"Frost has been here. They say it was a hiker. Frost seemed frightened."

They looked at each other for a moment. Harrison shrugged.

"That's all they will find. Has Frost gone?"

"Yes. He wanted to see you. He's coming back. But what if Duncan was behind the finding of that body? You expected him here this morning, but he hasn't come. He may have discovered something. You told me to be careful not to talk to him, that you'd once had trouble with him."

"I also told you I will attend to him. You needn't worry. He and the police can dig all they wish and they won't find anything. I haven't left a single loose thread hanging out."

"Well, they've got the gipsy."

"Who won't talk. They haven't got anything on him but a bit of smuggled brandy. What's that? Nothing. Do you think he is going to be such a fool as to talk about anything else? And Frost won't talk. He's in too deep to split."

"What about Grunevald?"

"Don't worry about him either. I tell you I have control of every factor in this game and I'm going to play it to the end. Raas was the only one who might split, and he'll never talk again."

"Well, they've found him too."

"What's the odds. That won't help them. They'll suspect some one from Little Soham. Let them. If things get too hot I'll throw them a bone."

"How?"

"Well, if the worst comes to the worst. I might even pin something on this stray Arab who has been hanging around. At any rate, it's time he was dealt with. He has been hovering about the place ever since Raas went."

"And Sir James Pinder?"

Harrison shrugged.

"What can he say? Don't you get the breeze up, my dear girl."

"You know I am not. I'm simply trying to anticipate difficulties. It paid you in Paris to listen to me. I repeat, I don't like the way things are going. I wish you could wind them up and let us get away from here."

"You won't have long to wait. I'm nearly ready now. I'll deal with Prince Faud to-night, if possible. As soon as I finish with him we can make the break. And now, let me see this fellow. While he is with me I want you to get ready to do your part. When I press the button you can come in with the tray. On your way to the desk do your stuff. Understand?

She, nodded, and now her greenish eyes were alight with a strange excitement. Under Harrison's soothing words her doubts had vanished. She was half French of the slums, half Parisian apache, and that half showed itself in her unwinking stare before she nodded and turned away.

She left the room, and Harrison transferred himself to Grunevald's chair. For the purposes of the interview he would pose as the doctor. The visitor wouldn't know the difference.

Scarcely was he settled when the door opened again and the Arab was ushered in. One of such apologetic manner and unhappy mien certainly did not look very formidable.

Whatever his purpose might be, Harrison was anxious enough to discover it. He had heard from several sources, chiefly from the gipsy tinker and from Frost the fisherman, that a dark foreigner was hanging about, and that he was staying at The Dog and Pheasant, in Ockham. He had decided that the fellow must be linked with Prince Faud, that he might be a danger, therefore, and that he must be dealt with soon. He could not have asked for a better chance than this to carry out his purpose. For Dr. Harrison was savagely determined that nothing should stand in the way of the successful consummation of this the biggest and richest prize for which he had ever schemed.

He received the stranger pleasantly enough. He bade him be seated in English, but when the other poured out a flood of Arabic, Harrison held up his hand.

"You do not speak my tongue?" he asked in the Cairene Arabic which he spoke very well, and which is closely akin to Syrian Arabic.

"May Allah forgive my stupidity, effendi, but I know only the tongue of the prophet. But the effendi has been blessed by Allah, for he speaks it as one of the chosen."

"Enough perhaps for us to converse," was Harrison's modest response. "Your card tells me that you are Hussein ben Mustapha of El Wejh. Why do you wish to see me?"

"Effendi, I will tell you all, for such is ordained. I have the honour to be regarded with some trust by His

Highness the Sheik of El Bakr, Sheereef of El Wejh, whose son, the Excellency Prince Faud, has come under the care of the illustrious effendi. It is for the purpose of watching over His Excellency's welfare and making a report to his father that Allah ordained that I should come to this land. Until two or three days ago His Excellency's personal attendant, Dr. Raas, gave me the news I sought. But now he does not come and my heart is anxious, for I know not what to say to the Sheik El Bakr. That is why I have come to the effendi to lift this burden from my heart. The effendi will not refuse permission for me to make salaam before His Excellency so that I may send news to the distant one that his heart may rejoice."

"Not at all," Harrison assured him. "You shall see him presently and judge for yourself how well he progresses. But first I would have you tell me where you met Dr. Raas? I am at a loss to know why he left us as he did. Can you tell me if he has gone back to his own land?"

"Effendi, it seems that he fell amongst thieves and murderers, for his body lies in one of the cities not far away. Even I, Hussein ben Mustapha, was seized and carried into this place and stood before the couch upon which the body lay. The caliph's men did question me, and I did answer truthfully, saying, verily, this is indeed the one who came out of the land of Araby with His Excellency the young Prince."

Harrison's eyes grew suddenly wary, but the gloam was hidden beneath lowered lids. This was news to him. He did not know that this stray Arab had been picked up by the local police and taken along to identify Raas's body. Mary Trent was right. He must watch his step. And the admission he had just heard determined him more than ever to put this prying Arab where the police couldn't question him a second time.

"What you tell me is strange news," he said after a pause. "I believed that Dr. Raas had left us because he was not happy in this part. I can understand now why you are anxious to know about Prince Faud. I shall arrange at once for you to see him."

With that Harrison pressed a button on the desk, and in a few minutes there was a knock at the door. It opened to admit the same trim maid. She carried the small silver tray which she had borne before, and at a sign from Harrison she came towards the desk.

The Arab was sitting with his back to the door, but as she approached he shifted his body a little and turned his head to look.

It was this movement that brought his face in position to receive fully and directly the charge of vapour that Mary Trent shot from a small gas pistol that was concealed beneath the tray.

He gasped and made one violent effort to get to his feet, but before he could do so, the gas had paralysed every nerve in his body, and he pitched forward at her feet, an inert mass.

Peter was not fool enough to hurl himself in wasted effort against a barrier that, he knew, would resist all such attacks.

After that first crash in which the man outside had beaten him to it, he drew back in the darkness of the concealed cockpit and waited until the stream of low curses had run into silence.

His mind was working fast. It was not difficult for him to guess something of the meaning of what had just happened. It had been plain to him, as soon as he uncovered the camouflaged engine, that the dilapidated-looking hulk was a very different craft from what she appeared—that, in fact, she was none other than the mysterious and powerful speed-boat that had come in from the sea the night before to disappear up French Creek.

Duncan's theory had not been at fault. He had told Peter to go to French Creek and try to locate such a craft but not even Duncan could have anticipated that the

unknown persons who operated this strange night service
would go to such pains to disguise their boat.

His discovery had told him, too, that he had found the
actual means by which contraband brandy was being
brought into the country, though he still hadn't the ghost
of a notion how Duncan connected this with the murder
at the Martello Tower, or the presence of Prince Faud at
Dr. Grunevald's sanatorium.

He guessed shrewdly, though, that in some way
Duncan did make a connection which included Harrison,
and of course he himself was aware of a definite link
between Harrison and Lee, the gipsy tinker, who
undoubtedly was one means of delivering the contraband
to various buyers.

He was uncertain, however, who it was that had
arrived on board at such an inopportune moment, though
he suspected it was some one directly associated in the
smuggling game. Duncan had mentioned the fisherman
from Little Soham whose movements had excited his
curiosity on various occasions, but Peter had seen him at
work on his boat in Little Soham when he had paused
there to see how the land lay. He realised, of course, that
there had been time for the man to follow to French
Creek by the river way had he so wished, but the brief
view Peter had had of him crouched in the outer cockpit
had been too indefinite for him to gather many details.

Whoever the other might be, he had acted with a
speed and determination that showed he was connected
with the boat in a proprietary way. Whether he knew
Peter's identity or of his connection with Hugh Duncan,
the lad couldn't tell. But the intensity of those curses was
sufficient to warn him that he was in a dangerous
situation.

He leant against the engine, and when the profanity
ceased, listened for the other's next move. For some
minutes there was utter silence, but he did not delude
himself into thinking that the man had gone.

Peter deliberately made a noise that could be heard outside. With a swiftness that held him frozen in his place there came a thud on the panel and a cold, threatening voice called:

"Keep quiet in there! I've got a shotgun here, and I'll fill you with both charges if you try any tricks."

Peter figured that his captor was not quite certain what to do with him, and in this he was right. The fisherman Frost, who had come up French Creek in the speed-boat that he used for his open and lawful purposes, was trying to decide on some plan. It would be simple enough to push the muzzle of the gun into the inner cockpit and blow a hole in his prisoner, but such a course threatened complications which he did not relish.

In his dilemma his mind turned to the man whose will had dominated him, as well as others, since his arrival at Dr. Grunevald's. He had better report to him, Frost told himself, and see what he thought about his prisoner.

Harrison had told him that he must watch this boy and his employer, that they were a danger to him. Whatever the answer, Frost knew that he must keep the secret of the hulk from leaking out.

Reaching this decision, he debated whether to make certain of his captive or to leave him as he was. Rising, he went along the deck to where his other boat lay tied to the stern of the hulk, and hauled it close. In the hold beneath, Peter could hear his footsteps as well as feel the roll of the boat as it yielded to his movements. He was hoping that his captor would leave him for the time being, for he was certain that he could soon find something lying about that could be used for smashing a way out.

But that hope was doomed to disappointment when he heard the footsteps returning.

"You, in there," Frost growled. "I'm going to open up. I want you to come out. I'll have you covered. If you try any monkey tricks I'll blow you to pieces."

There was something in the tone of the voice that told Peter he must take no chances. So, quietly enough, he walked out, bent down so as to pass the outer cockpit, and in doing so realised that now he had the nearest thing to a chance he would get.

He tensed his muscles swiftly, bent down a little more, and was on the point of launching himself at the other when Frost smashed the muzzle end of the gun on his head. Peter never knew what struck him. It was a simple enough matter for Frost to bind him and heave him on to one of the piles of casks.

Abel Frost returned in his speed-boat to Little Soham and within ten minutes was inside Dr. Grunevald's sanatorium. He was taken at once to Dr Grunevald's private room, and there he found the doctor's new partner ready to listen to what he had to report, and to give him instructions as to what he should do next.

"It may be some casual Nosy Parker," he told Frost, "but I've a hunch it may be some one entirely different. If I am right, you run him out to sea a few miles and dump him."

Abel Frost did not answer at once. In one short week things had changed entirely for him. He was afraid, though neither he nor Harrison knew that Hugh Duncan was on the point of finding the body of Peel. Harrison read his mental attitude well enough.

"Getting cold feet, are you?" he sneered. "Well—don't. You're in this thing, and you are going to stay."

Abel Frost lifted his blue eyes and stared into those of the man opposite to him.

"I think we understand each other," Harrison went on pleasantly. "If you have any lingering doubts, then you had better see Dr. Grunevald. He would tell you that the only course is to obey my instructions to the letter."

Frost muttered something unintelligible, but Harrison guessed its purport.

"You're thinking about what was found in the sand by the Martello Tower. Don't worry about that. I'll tell you something. This fellow Duncan will soon be in my hands. I've arranged things so that he will walk into a trap. If that bird you have caged at French Creek is his assistant, it is the best thing that could have happened. You clear off now. Be here early this evening. I'll have definite instructions for you then. I shall want to have a look at your catch."

With that, Frost took his departure.

But the morning wore away without Duncan arriving at the sanatorium. The afternoon came and went, and still he did not appear. And, just after dusk, an Arab figure was the only one to arrive. How he was dealt with is already known.

CHAPTER TWELVE

By nine o'clock that evening Harrison was in a quandary.

He knew well enough now that the body of Detective-Sergeant Peel had been found, and despite his airy assurances to Mary Trent, he was by no means easy in his mind.

It was plain enough that at an hour when he thought Hugh Duncan would be walking into his trap, the private inquiry agent had been busy investigating the abandoned limekilns some miles away.

The actual fact of the discovery of the body was not as disturbing to Harrison as the puzzle of how Duncan had known where to look; for he was quite convinced that it was through Duncan and none other that the search had been made in that particular spot. He had summed him up correctly when they had met in India, and he feared him. Besides, apart from his experience of him in India, his carefully prepared priming in the form of the letter had missed fire somehow. Duncan must have had some sort of definite lead to go on. Harrison realised that such a lead might be quite meaningless to the local police. Indeed, everything had gone without a single hitch while he had had only them to deal with; but somehow in the last two days or so there had been irritating complications—a period of time that coincided with Duncan's presence in the district. The inference was only too obvious.

He was waiting now for a report on which he might be able to act. If Duncan was at the inn at Benham, then Harrison had decided to handle matters himself. If not, then he would locate him as soon as possible and deal with him in the same effective manner. As for Duncan's assistant, if the fellow whom Abel Frost had trapped aboard his boat were he, then that end of it, too, would be easy.

In any event that pair must be disposed of, for the game was reaching a climax now, and he didn't intend that a couple of detectives should spoil it.

He was alone in Grunevald's private room when Mary Trent came in. She closed the door carefully and came close to the desk before she spoke.

"Fitzy is back," she told him in a low tone. The man she referred to as "Fitzy" was an American gunman whom Harrison had picked up and brought along with him—the same who had taken the major part in the attempt to kill Duncan in the car.

"What does he say?"

"He's been at the inn. He found he had to make the inquiry quite openly. The landlord admits that Duncan is there, but says he left strict orders that he was not to be disturbed on any account, not even if the police inspector came."

"I wonder what he's up to?"

"Something that is no good to us, you may be sure."

"I'll bet you're right enough there."

"I don't like it, old boy. If we don't look out we'll find the whole place overrun with police. If that happens you won't be able to count on any one but me."

"But it won't happen, my dear. I'll attend to Duncan myself."

"How?"

"You leave that to me. I'm only waiting for Frost to turn up."

"He's here. He came in just after Fitzy."

"Good. Bring him along to me."

She nodded and left the room by the other door. Within a few moments she was back, with Frost following her. She did not leave the room while Harrison questioned Frost.

"Everything all right?"

"It was when I left French Creek at eight o'clock."

"You had a good look at him?"

"Yes. He was lying just where I put him."

"Good. I'm going along to have a look at him. Then I'm going on to Benham. I want you to be standing by ready to run out to sea. I shall be going with you. I expect we shall have another passenger as well."

"Is that all?"

The question was in a sulky tone, and Mary Trent glanced at Frost sharply. As for Harrison, he was out of his chair with such amazing speed that the fisherman had no more time to make a startled movement before Harrison's hands were at his throat.

Frost was not a big man, but he was of exceptional strength, which he exerted savagely against Harrison's attack. But within twenty seconds he was flat on his back with Harrison astride him, his hands still on his throat in a throttling grip.

When Harrison rose it was to drag up with him a figure that was so limp that it sagged in his grasp. In those few moments he had reduced Abel Frost to a flabby wreck.

"One more break like that and I'll leave you out at sea too," he snarled. "Now, get out and wait for me."

He threw the other from him, and Frost, keeping his balance with an effort, managed to get out of the room. Mary Trent nodded approvingly.

"He needed that warning," she said. "I didn't like his manner this morning. He looked as if he were cracking."

"The only cracking he'll do is what I give him," growled Harrison. "I'm going to French Creek now, then I'm going to Benham. I don't know what time I'll be back, but while I'm gone I want you to keep an eye on Grunevald, and it won't do any harm to take a look at Sir James Pinder as well. If he wants to see Prince Faud, let him. You know how to listen in. I want to keep tabs on what goes on while I'm not here."

"Leave it to me. But—watch your step when you get to Benham."

Harrison grinned as he rose.

"Give me a stiff brandy before I go, Mary,"

He drove himself in his own car, as far as it was possible to approach the camouflaged boat on French Creek. Where he pulled up to proceed on foot, he was close to the spot where Peter had left his motor-cycle.

Abel Frost had led the way on his machine, and now the two walked silently along the top of the embankment towards the dark hulk which was their objective.

The night was clear and starry.

As they approached close, they could see the outline of the boat where it lay by the bank. Not a light showed. It looked utterly desolate and abandoned.

Frost led the way aboard, and then forward to the cockpit. Harrison followed. When both were in the cockpit Harrison switched on a pocket torch and held it while Frost released the panel that gave access to the inner secret engine-room.

Now, at a sign from the fisherman, Harrison took the lead. He moved towards the narrow opening that gave access to the hold beyond, and, standing there, thrust his arm through so that the beam of light lit up the whole place.

For a moment or two he stood thus with Frost just behind him. Then Harrison withdrew his arm, and turned slowly so that his eyes were close to Frost's.

"You say you left your prisoner in there?" he asked in a voice that was dangerously calm.

"Yes, just as I told you."

"Well, then, perhaps you will produce him, for unless he's inside one of those casks he isn't in that hold."

A startled oath broke from Frost. He started forward, and Harrison did not protest when he reached for the torch. Then Harrison stood aside so that the other could squeeze through into the inner hold. He watched him while he sent the beam of light stabbing high and low and from side to side, smiled sardonically while he even moved some of the casks as though he expected to find his vanished prisoner beneath them. Finally he turned.

"I—I don't understand," he gasped. Harrison laughed harshly.

"Of course you don't, you dumb egg," he jeered. "You couldn't understand anything so plain. But I do, and I'll enlighten you. Some one has rescued your prisoner. Is that plain enough? And, if you were telling the truth when you said you left him here at eight o'clock, then his escape has been effected within the past two hours."

"But how—"

"Don't stand there asking fool questions. I don't need to see him to know his identity. You stay here and be ready to put to sea the moment I return. I've got a job to do, and it won't take me long."

With that, Harrison flung out of the cockpit on to the deck. He almost ran along the top of the embankment, so anxious was he to reach the car. His one thought was to reach Benham as soon as possible.

He was certain now that the prisoner had been Duncan's assistant. No casual passer-by whose inquisitiveness had led him into trouble would have been released so mysteriously.

At first sight it had been impossible to tell that the panel had been opened. But it must have been removed from the outside and replaced after the prisoner had been released. Had he been just any casual who had been rescued by another passer-by, then it stood to reason that the panel would simply have been smashed in and left as it was.

No, this rescue had been effected by some one who had known how to remove the panel in the proper way. Unless this person was already cognisant of the secret, then he must have been instructed by the prisoner. That meant, to Harrison's mind, a combination of Duncan and his assistant.

If his theory was right, then he must move swiftly. Duncan had digged more deeply than he thought. He—Harrison—had felt satisfied that, if he kept out of sight, Duncan would never suspect what was going on under the cloak of high respectability that hung over the Grunevald sanatorium.

The discovery of the body of Dr. Raas had not perturbed him very much. There was nothing there, he felt confident, to be linked up with him. The more recent finding of Peel's body, however, had been a sharp warning. That could not have been due to chance.

Harrison had been willing to believe that Lee had been pulled in by the police through betrayal by some local person. He knew country districts were saturated with petty jealousies that often took vicious forms of expression. And not a whisper had leaked out that there was anything more against Lee than being in possession of smuggled spirits.

Yet Peel's body had been found. Lee could have told where it lay, but Harrison did not believe he had been such a fool. To make such an admission would be as good as to put a noose round his neck, whereas to take the knock over a few kegs of smuggled spirits might mean no more than confiscation and fine, or, at worst, a very short term in quod.

Yes, now that the prisoner whom Frost had caught was gone, the more he thought it over, the more convinced Harrison became that it was Duncan's man, and that the rescue had been engineered by Duncan; which, if it were so, meant that Duncan had discovered far more than Harrison had believed possible, and thereby had signed his death-warrant. For Dr. Harrison was playing for such a colossal prize this time that half a dozen lives were not to stand in his way. Besides, he owed the other a grudge. Duncan had very nearly tripped him up at that trial.

By the time he was on the outskirts of Benham he had formed a plan to deal with the immediate problem. He figured that if Duncan had rescued his assistant from the boat on French Creek, then, for the lad's sake at least— Frost had told him how he had smashed the lad unconscious—Duncan would return to Benham.

Harrison regretted now that he had not brought Fitzy with him. He would have been more than useful if it came to shooting it out with the pair. On the other hand, he himself had another weapon that, if he could come to close quarters with his quarry, would be quite as effective, swift, and far more silent than an ordinary gun.

He drove the car into a narrow side road just before the turn that would reveal the main village street. Then, making sure that his weapon was handy to his need, he proceeded on foot.

He knew his way to the inn. Harrison was not one to operate in a district without making himself familiar with it. And he knew the police station. The only notice he took of it as he passed was to twist his lips into a sneer. They didn't keep him awake of nights.

But when he saw the lights of the inn, red through the drawn blinds, he gave all his attention to what lay ahead.

He was perfectly aware of the location of Duncan's rooms, and of the fact that they could be reached without going through the inn proper.

It was his intention to approach by this way first, and not to appear inside the inn unless circumstances forced him to do so.

He found a narrow alley that would take him around the inn to a small wicket gate that gave into the garden.

He followed this. Not a soul did he meet, nor had he met any one since entering the village.

He found the gate and slipped into the garden. To the left he could see the lights of the inn kitchen, and from somewhere beyond came the inane laugh of some labourer.

Harrison turned to the right, and found himself close to the windows which he knew to be those of Duncan's rooms. Not a light showed. He crouched down close to one and listened. Not a sound came to him.

He crept along to another which, he figured, would be that of the sitting-room. Still darkness and silence. He continued to the third just beyond which was the corner of the building. The same conditions met him here.

His eyes narrowed as he straightened up and went back to the second window. He stood here listening again for some minutes, but no movement of any sort reached him from within.

Harrison took out a small flat instrument that slipped easily enough under the ancient frame of the lower sash. He levered it gently, and found that the sash lifted freely. He thrust his fingers beneath it and raised it high enough to permit his body to squeeze through.

But he did not proceed at once. Instead, he swung quickly to one side, and, with his gas pistol ready, waited. He knew that Duncan was quite capable of leaving an easy approach for him to step into a trap.

But no trap was sprung. The only movement was the slight stirring of the curtains as the draught caught them and billowed them in and out.

Then Harrison took the plunge. His movements were silent and extraordinarily agile for a man of his size. No one standing more than a few feet away would have seen the swift shadow through the window.

Leaving the window open for quick retreat if necessary, Harrison took out his torch and flashed the beam round the room. He found that he had been right in his placing of the rooms. This was a small sitting-room, cosily enough furnished. There were plenty of signs that it was in occupation; but, at the moment, the occupant, whoever he might be, was certainly not visible. The chairs were empty, and so was the couch. A small fire burned in the grate, and there was a peculiar odour in the air that for the moment Harrison could not place.

He stepped quickly to a door on his left. It opened, as he thought, into a bedroom. There was some luggage, but no human occupant. His business now wasn't with luggage, so, closing the door, he crossed the sitting room and peered into another and smaller bedroom. It, too, was empty of human presence; but there was more luggage about, belonging, he guessed swiftly, to the boy.

He retreated into the sitting-room and continued his examination there. He was wondering at the same time if his quarry might be out in one of the bars.

He was telling himself that, somewhere, his reasoning was at fault. He could not understand the two returning to the inn and not being found in their rooms, for Frost had been very definite about the force of the blow he had dealt his prisoner. The only conclusion that seemed possible was that some urgent business had kept them on the move. But what? A feeling of uneasiness that was new to him came over Harrison. He sensed a lot of work going on under cover of which he should be aware, but wasn't.

Then, suddenly, his probing gaze fell on something on the table. It was an ordinary enough domestic utensil, no more than a white plate with a fork and spoon beside it.

But it wasn't the utensils that held Harrison's frowning attention. It was the few crumbs of food that remained upon the plate, for he was prepared to lay very long odds that neither Duncan nor his assistant would request such food to be served in a country inn no matter to what extent they might consume it under certain other conditions.

Yet the remains indicated a simple enough meal. There appeared to be only a few grains of rice with something reddish in colour mixed among them.

Tomato? Harrison stepped closer and investigated more closely. No, that reddish matter wasn't tomato sauce. It was the remains of some chilies. Rice and chilies. Who had been eating that distinctively Eastern dish in an English inn?

For some moments Harrison stood rigid, staring down at the plate while his mind worked fast. No detective could have applied the laws of analysis and deduction more efficiently than Dr. Harrison. It was this faculty possibly that had enabled him so often to counter police moves.

His mind leapt to Prince Faud and to Dr. Raas. Prince Faud could not have been here to partake of this dish, which was one of the common foods of his own country. He was locked up safely enough at the sanatorium.

Nor could Dr. Raas have wielded that fork and spoon, for he was as dead as mutton. Then who?

There was that stray Arab fellow who had been hanging about the district for some days, and who had appeared at the sanatorium not more than three hours ago.

Could he be the one who had sat at this plate? If so, then it meant that he had been in direct contact with Duncan, a contact that had been sufficiently prolonged for Duncan to go to the pains of procuring him food that he would find palatable. For Harrison knew that some trouble had been taken to arrange for rice and chilies to be served in this way at a country inn.

An even more startling suggestion flashed into his mind. Perhaps Duncan had deliberately sent the fellow to the sanatorium. That might explain why there had been no apparent response to the letter of Sir James Pinder's that had been so carefully planted. Evidently Duncan had not fallen for that, but had evolved a counter stroke.

Harrison backed away and stood wary, as if he expected to be rushed at any moment. Then he moved quietly towards the window. He slipped through it as quietly as he had entered, and paused long enough to draw the sash as he had found it.

He streaked through the garden and along the alley like a shadow. He did not take the trouble to look into the bars. He strode down the street without meeting a soul, but when he was outside the village he drew up with a low oath, for another suggestion had struck him with the force of a violent electric shock.

He began to run now. It seemed that he could not get into the car quickly enough since this latest possibility had come to him. His course back to the sanatorium was so reckless as to betray the agitation in his mind.

He left the car at the front door, and using his own key to enter, strode along towards the private office.

But before reaching the door, a figure glided out of the shadows. It was Mary Trent. She caught his arm and began to whisper.

"I'm so glad you've come. I've had a look at that Arab, but he isn't an Arab at all. It's—"

"I know," he interrupted her savagely. "I know who it is. It's Hugh Duncan."

CHAPTER THIRTEEN

PETER'S release from the camouflaged bulk was as mysterious to him as it was surprising to Duncan.

It had taken a long time for him to grasp his position when he had recovered consciousness after the savage blow his captor had dealt him, but eventually he remembered those last conscious moments when he had decided to seize the very slim chance that offered and make a dive for it. Well, he had been beaten to it, so there was no use whining over that.

Then, slowly, he identified the overpowering atmosphere as that of strong spirits. Indeed, so saturated was the confined air of the place with the reek that this in itself was almost enough to becloud his senses. On the other hand, unknown to him, it was the very potency of the fumes that had brought him back to consciousness.

He could not make even the foggiest guess as to time. The hold was in utter darkness. Outside it might be day or night, he could not tell. He did not even know whether the boat had been under way while he lay as one dead, or whether it was still moored to the bank in French Creek.

But of one thing he did feel assured—his captor would return eventually.

While his brain struggled to reason coherently, he experienced an ever-growing thirst that rose to a pitch of maddening desire. He knew that within a few feet of him was water, not the salty flow of French Creek but the ditchwater that found its way across the marshes. Even that would have been to him now as the most delicious draught, but it was as impossible to reach as an icy spring in the Alps, so he turned and twisted while the agony grew almost unendurable.

It was after an eternity of time that a sound caught his ear. Then the boat dipped suddenly, and he knew some one had stepped aboard. There followed the thud of heels overhead. He could follow their course while they approached the cockpit.

His ears strained so hard now that for the moment his thirst was forgotten. He could detect the rattle of the panel that gave access to the secret cockpit, then the shuffle of footsteps came nearer and nearer, and suddenly a beam of light struck him full in the face.

Peter closed his eyes and lay still. He could not have seen any definite form behind the screen of that light. He knew that if it was a friend he would soon be released; if it was his captor again, then he might as well appear to be still unconscious.

He soon knew it was the latter. There came a grunt, the light was turned away, and the intruder stamped back as he had come. Peter opened his eyes, but could only see a dim bulk outlined against the glare. Then the light vanished as the cockpit panel was slammed back into place, and the steps again came along the deck, the boat giving another lurch as their owner sprang ashore.

One thing he did gain from that visit, and that was the knowledge that it was night, for not a shaft of daylight had penetrated from the outside. It told him, too, that his captor had some reason for keeping tabs on him.

Did that mean that his identity was known? If so, then his position was as dangerous as possible. He thought of Duncan. Where was he? Had he paid his intended visit to the sanatorium? If so, what had been the result?

Peter reasoned that if it was now night, Duncan must have been worried for some time about his prolonged absence. If he were, then it was safe betting that he would start out to look for him. In that case why hadn't he arrived before now? Duncan knew that he—Peter— had gone to French Creek. It could be taken for granted that Duncan would detect the camouflage of the contraband boat as quickly as his assistant, and that would mean immediate investigation, with the discovery of Peter's predicament. But none of this had happened. Why? Where was Duncan? Or wasn't he worrying yet?

In the midst of his effort to find some hope in the situation, a new sound caught Peter's ear. The boat gave another lurch, but far less violent than before. It was a more gentle dipping, as though some weight had pressed upon the gunwale very gently. It recovered its level, and, twisting his head painfully so as to hear better, Peter made out a sound that was more of a continuous shuffle than anything else. It was the sort of noise a good-sized animal might have made in prowling along the deck.

Then silence. The person or thing, whichever it was, had come to a stop, and the stillness was as heavy as ever.

Peter knew perfectly well that his captor would never board his own boat in that fashion. A wild hope came to him that it was Duncan making a cautious investigation. If it was, then he must let him know where he was.

He opened his mouth to shout. To his amazement, no more than a gasp twisted his throat painfully. He tried again and again, each time forcing the swollen muscles to obey his will a little more. Then in one desperate effort he managed to emit what sounded to him no more than a hoarse croak.

He listened. Not a sound reached him. He gathered himself together and made another effort. This time his voice burst out with more volume, and, an idea occurring to him, he began to lift his feet up so that he could beat his heels down upon one of the casks.

The noise itself was not much, but in that confined space the acoustic properties were just what was needed to turn it into a drumming sound.

He paused. Now he could hear noises again on deck; then came a sharp hammering almost directly over his head. He found voice once more.

"I'm here! H-e-r-e," he tried to yell. "Down in the hold."

He heard further tapping, which puzzled him. If it were Duncan, why didn't he reply?

He knew that there was a hatch-cover over the hold, for it was there he had found the bit of dottle. But it had looked to him to be fastened very securely, and he did not think it could be opened without heavy tools and much trouble—a big risk to take now, for his captor might be returning at any moment.

It was evident that the man above was having a go at it, however, for Peter heard further tappings that seemed to indicate this. He found that the excitement engendered by the prospect of release had given him back his voice almost in full volume. Now he used it to some purpose.

"Hey!" he yelled. "There's an easier way in than that. If you walk aft, you'll find the open cockpit. There's a secret panel there, the front one. It opens into this hole."

He paused, expecting to hear Duncan reply, but, to his amazement, a very different voice reached him. It was slow, and its owner was obviously finding great difficulty in finding the necessary words.

"You explain me better," Peter heard faintly, the sound being muffled by the intervening deck.

"It isn't the chief," he muttered in disappointment. "But if it is some bloke that will let me out of this, it is almost as good."

So he shouted again, speaking slowly and very distinctly. He managed at last, it seemed, to make the unseen person of good intent understand what he was driving at, for the shuffling footsteps went along the deck, and then he could hear distant sounds of fumbling at the cockpit panel.

A draught of cool air was the first thing that told Peter the other had got the panel open. He called cautiously. A voice answered him in the darkness.

"Don't light a match," Peter warned. "This air here is dangerous."

The other murmured something, and apparently continued to approach, for the sounds became more distinct. Then Peter's heart jumped as something touched his leg.

Whoever his rescuer was, he acted swiftly and efficiently now that he had reached Peter. He removed the boy's bonds and rubbed his tortured wrists and ankles with hands that were not new to the work. Indeed, those same hands had secured bonds as well as loosened them, in the wild life of the Arabian desert.

Peter was impatient to be gone, but he knew it would be impossible for him to walk until the blood was flowing again, so he restrained his impatience until the other gave a soft grunt and helped him to the floor.

Peter did not forget the precaution of leaving mystery behind him. He collected the bits of rope and stuffed them into his pockets, and when he was in the cockpit he replaced the panel carefully. Then as they climbed out on to the deck, he was able by the faint light of the stars to get his first glimpse of his rescuer.

Duncan had mentioned the fact that there was a mysterious Arab hanging about Ockham. Peter, of course, knew nothing of Hussein ben Mustapha and his visit to the inn at Benham; nor of what had taken place since, for he had left for French Creek before the Arab's arrival, but it seemed a reasonable guess that this fellow was either the same whom Duncan had seen at Ockham, or one of the same tribe; though how he happened to be prowling about such .a lonely spot at this hour of the night was a mystery.

This was not the time, however, to stop for questions. He had been released in an entirely unexpected way, and now all he wanted was to get to his motor-cycle and find Duncan as quickly as possible.

To his astonishment, his companion seemed to divine his thoughts. He waved a hand towards the embankment.

"The steed on wheels, effendi," he said, in his difficult English, "it is gone. There is no way but that of the dateseller." This, Peter learnt later, meant they must proceed on foot.

"I must get to Benham," he said slowly. "It is a long distance."

"I come too with the effendi to the caravanserai, there to await the return of Duncan effendi."

"Well, I'm darned," muttered Peter. Then aloud, "Did he send you to find me?"

"No, effendi. I was passing, as I pass often at night in this land. But better we make haste. The effendi's enemies may return."

With that he seemed to be overcome by his effort at English, for he relapsed into silence, and together they strode across the marshes, Peter discovering to his further amazement that his companion knew the most direct way as only one long resident in the district could have known it.

They left Little Soham on the left. Peter was not anxious to be seen by any one there until he should have reported to Duncan what had happened. He was confident now that his captor had been Frost.

At this moment, away to the right, he saw the lights of a car that was approaching along the road from Ockham. He wondered if it had any connection with himself or Duncan. It had. It was Harrison coming to the hulk to find that he was gone.

Then they struck across Little Sahara. It was a journey that few local people would have been bold enough to attempt on a dark night, for there were many sinister tales about that desolate area—tales which those who used the Martello Tower for nefarious purposes were careful to keep alive. It was the best protection they could have had, for no country policeman was any more anxious than the villagers to penetrate the place at night. This desire to shun it had become greatly intensified since the recent finding of a body by the tower. But its sinister name did not worry Peter, and his companion appeared quite unconcerned. Little Sahara had no terrors to compare with his own vast deserts, where predatory enemies hovered like eagles.

Had Peter known what was to happen during the time which he and Hussein took to cross from the Ockham road on one side of Little Sahara to the Benham road on the other, he would have risked being seen in Little Soham in order to try to secure some sort of motor vehicle to take them, but he believed that he would find Duncan on his arrival and, indeed, so did his companion, for Hussein thought that by then Duncan would have finished at the sanatorium.

On his way, by means of Hussein's limited English, they managed to carry on some sort of conversation which eventually told Peter something of Duncan's movements.

He heard too, about the finding of another body, though the Arab could give him no idea of where it had been found or of the identity of the victim. He had an idea, however, that it had been some one connected with the same matters that had brought Duncan to this part of the country, and Peter asked himself if it could be the missing Peel.

It was while they were still moving across Little Sahara that Dr. Harrison made his visits to the inn at Benham, to find no one in Duncan's rooms but a clue, in the form of rice and chilies on a plate, which had sent him racing back to the sanatorium.

He had been gone some time when the fagged Peter stumbled into the front door of the inn and learned from the landlord that he had not seen Duncan since he locked himself in his rooms some hours earlier.

"Not a soul has been in there, sir," he assured Peter. "As a matter of fact, I'm glad you've come, for he must be getting hungry."

He knew nothing of Duncan's departure disguised as an Arab, nor of Hussein's subsequent departure through the window, any more than he knew of Harrison's visit an hour before.

Peter saw nothing to tell him that some one had been in the rooms since Duncan's departure, but the Arab at once caught his arm and pointed towards the table: "Look! Mr. Duncan has not returned, but there have been some one here. Hands have moved the the eating things on that plate. They are not as I leave them."

CHAPTER FOURTEEN

"WHAT do you mean?"

Peter dragged Hussein to the table and urged him to explain his words. The Arab pointed out the few differences which enabled him to know that some one had certainly moved the plate and the fork and spoon upon it since he had been there. He was positive he had left them in such a fashion, as was his regular habit. Now they were differently placed

Peter accepted his reasoning. He hadn't by any means taken to this queer bird that Duncan had picked up, but he was already beginning to suspect that the Arab was no one's fool, and certainly he—Peter—owed him civil attention at least in view of the signal service he had done him that night.

He debated the possibility of Duncan having returned and left again. That did not seem reasonable. First, Duncan had gone out disguised as an Arab. The landlord had taken him for the stranger who had returned with Peter. Had some one of his appearance come in before he would have noticed the fact and mentioned it. Besides, he was quite positive that no one had approached Duncan's rooms.

There was, of course, the further possibility that Duncan had come and gone by the window, but, if so, what had brought him back and taken him out again without any message for Peter?

Peter entered each bedroom and gave it a swift scrutiny. Both appeared normal in every way. He made a second tour of the sitting-room which in its course brought him to the window. He lifted the sash and sent the beam of his torch outside. It was Hussein who first discovered signs that some one had been moving about on the ground beneath. To eyes that had been trained to read the faint signs of the desert these marks were as plain as print.

"Some one has been standing here," he said, as he pointed out the course the marks followed. "A big man stood beneath each window."

Peter nodded quickly.

"You're right. And it is the same person who has been inside. Look here!"

He pointed to the marks that had been left by the fiat instrument with which Harrison had forced up the sash.

"He wasn't any too particular about covering his track either. This is the way our bird came and left."

Hussein did not understand half the words Peter used, but he gathered the meaning well enough. Together they made their way from the window to the gate, following the way Harrison had come and gone as certainly as if they had had his actual presence as a guide. Then they returned to the sitting-room.

"Well, that's that," muttered Peter, staring at the plate on the table. "Now who was it? It certainly wasn't the chief. He would have no reason to fiddle with that plate. But why was the person who did touch it so interested in it? There is something queer about this. Was it some one from the sanatorium? It is the sort of thing that Dr. Harrison might do, according to the chief's warnings about him. But why? Have they spotted the chief's disguise? Has that something to do with it? At any rate he went there, and as far as I can figure, he must still be there. It looks to me as though my best bet is to find out what has happened in that direction."

Suddenly he turned to his silent companion. Hussein was gazing at the floor.

"What do you think about this?" Peter asked him, with a wave of the hand.

"A vicious camel. Mr. Duncan has not returned here. He has gone to the palace where is my master's son. It is there that the vicious camel will strike. We must go there. We must hurry. My master's son is there. I am—am—diseasy."

Peter regarded him curiously.

"You seem a pretty shrewd fellow," he told him in English. "How did you find me to-night?"

"That ship—it makes strange journeys in the darkness, but in the light of day it lies abandoned as a dead hulk. I have noticed it often—much. But we must hurry from here to the—the—palace."

Hussein was at Peter's heels when he left the inn by a side door and crossed the yard to the lockup garage which housed Duncan's car. A few minutes later they were racing through the night on their way to the sanatorium; while within the walls of that establishment strange and sinister drama was being played.

It had not taken Dr. Harrison long to reach the room into which the unconscious Duncan had been thrown. The pseudo Arab lay on a bed just as he had been dumped, for the shot of gas had done its work well.

Harrison bent over the unconscious form and satisfied himself that Mary Trent had made no mistake; then he sat down and looked at her.

"This alters everything," he said at last. "He was in far deeper than I suspected."

"He must have found out a lot to come here like this," she returned. "What are you going to do?"

"Does Grunevald know yet?"

"No. I haven't said a word to a soul. I was waiting for you to come back. If he had begun to recover consciousness I'd have given him another shot to keep him quiet."

"Good girl! He must have been behind the finding of Peel's body. But how? There hasn't been a leak of any sort."

"What about the tinker?"

"Impossible. Lee would never be such a fool. Besides, they don't third-degree a man in this country. He is quite

cunning enough to know that they haven't anything much
on him. No, Lee didn't blow the gaff."

"But some one must have put him wise. Or was there
something he could get hold of by nosing around?"

"Not a thing, I tell you."

"Well, what about Grunevald? Maybe he has cracked
and is double-crossing you."

"He wouldn't be such a fool. What would he have to
gain? Nothing. And he knows if anything did break he'd
be in as deep as any one. No, it wasn't Grunevald."

"Then whom? Is it possible that Sir James Pinder—"
Harrison interrupted her with an impatient gesture.

"I'm going to put that to the test to-night. Things have
got to be speeded up. This outside business has made it
necessary. I'm not worrying about the police, but that
confounded assistant of Duncan's is at large, and I'm
hanged if I know how he managed it. If I thought Frost
had been double-crossing me I'd know what to do, but the
fellow seemed honest enough in his denials. With Duncan
missing, his man will try to find out where he is. We must
be on the watch for him. The other danger is that he may
have the police poking their noses in here."

"Aren't they sure to do that when it is known that the
body found in the limekiln is Peel's?"

"Scotland Yard will throw a fit," agreed Harrison. "I'm
beginning to get a hunch that Duncan is down here on
their behalf. They must have been curious to know why
they didn't hear from Peel. But even so Duncan knows a
lot that I can't account for. He's found out something in
some way. He did before, you know."

"Well, we've got him."

"And we'll keep him until we're ready to dispose of
him. Just the same, I wanted more time. Grunevald
doesn't worry me. It's our dusky prince. I wanted to
handle him gently. He and Pinder between them have
what we want, and we've got to get it to-night."

"You mean you will wind things up so soon?"

"We've got to!" Harrison exploded. "There's the ransom of a kingdom at stake, and I'm not taking any chances. I've got the things all planned. If one bit doesn't fit, we'll discard it. I'm going to put Prince Faud and Pinder together again and see what happens."

Mary Trent glanced meaningly at the form on the bed. "What about him?"

"What do you mean? He's all right for the time being."

"If you are going to listen-in to those two, won't you want to move him?"

"Daren't. I mustn't be seen lugging a body about the place. You never know when some of these people of Grunevald's might blow the gaff to the police if they suspect he isn't a patient. They must have heard something about Raas and Peel. We'll let him stew where he is. He won't hear anything; that gas will hold him under. You wait here. If he does make a move, give him another shot but not too much. I shall want to talk to him before I finish."

Sir James Pinder was seated in a low chair, reading, when Harrison knocked and entered.

The room was an excellent example of how comfortably Dr. Grunevald installed the patients who came into residence at his exclusive sanatorium.

The furniture was just the sort that a man such as Sir James Pinder would choose for his own den. There was a long, inviting leather couch, two deep leather arm-chairs, good pictures, and packed bookcases rising half the height of each wall. A cheerful fire burned in the grate, and the light by which Sir James read was placed in exactly the right position. Through a half-open door one could just glimpse the bedroom beyond. If quiet and comfort were essentials to the welfare of a patient, then Sir James had them.

He laid aside his book as Harrison stepped in, and lifted his brows inquiringly. Harrison nodded genially, and sat down facing him.

"I am sorry to disturb you at this hour of the evening, Sir James, but it is essential to my plans. I am afraid I must ask you to be good enough to have another talk with Prince Faud."

The old archaeologist stroked his beard and peered at Harrison with shrewd eyes. Since his last interview with Prince Faud he understood Dr. Harrison.

"But why to-night?" he asked mildly. "What more do you expect me to discover than before. I have already told you that Prince Faud either knows nothing, or will not talk."

"I am afraid I must reply with a vulgar word, Sir James. It is bunkum."

"Your mode of expression will not alter facts, my dear doctor."

Harrison leant forward. His face had taken on hard lines, and his eyes showed the intensity of his purpose.

"Let us understand each other, Sir James. I have made no secret of my purpose. I know that Prince Faud came to this country with the sole purpose of making secret contact with you. His father, the Sheik El Bakr of El Wejh, is known to me personally."

"As a friend?"

"That is beside the point. It is sufficient that I know him, and know that he hasn't sent his son all this distance on a wild-goose chase. In fact, I was in Arabia when the idea was conceived. I know what is going on out there between Sheik El Bakr and the emir of the neighbouring state. El Bakr had found something in the desert. It was you who showed him that it was there to be found for the digging. It is something that has lain beneath those sands ever since the Queen of Sheba made her historic visit to King Solomon. It was on her return journey that her caravan halted there. No written history gives the details of that halt, but you know them because in your excavations you found tablets which told you. From those tablets you learned that of the Queen's enormous caravan of more than three thousand people, half were destroyed by the most terrific sandstorm that had ever been known. Am I right?"

"You talk most interestingly."

"You know that I am telling you facts. I'll give you more. For many days this great storm raged, and when it was over the caravan was only a remnant of the proud cavalcade that had been making its stately way across the desert. The Queen was safe, so were the more favoured of her followers, but so decimated was the total number that it was found essential to abandon half of the precious baggage which was being taken back to the queen's own country—half of the treasure that Solomon had given her."

"Indeed. . . ." murmured the other.

"It was her intention, after her arrival in Abyssinia, to send back a fresh caravan to retrieve this treasure, and so that the stuff might remain safe from marauders it was buried deep and covered with a stone structure. Centuries passed while that treasure lay undisturbed. The Queen of Sheba had found it impossible to send the caravan, for she was occupied with troubles at home. Then she died, taking the secret with her, and no one was actually sure that it was not only a story without foundation until Sir James Pinder, during the course of his excavations in that part of Arabia, unearthed a stone cairn which he found was the actual structure erected by the great queen. Is that right?"

"But no treasure, my dear doctor, no treasure." Harrison grinned savagely.

"Do you think I don't know that? Prince Faud wouldn't be in England if El Bakr had been able to lay his hands on it. But he doesn't know just where to look. Neither does his enemy, Emir El Birk. Only one person has discovered that in all the thousands of years it has lain there, and that person is—you!"

"Indeed! You attribute magical powers to me."

"Not in the least. Just as the Rosetta stone was found in Egypt which gave the key to the dead hieroglyphic language of the ancient Egyptians, so did you discover a stone slab cut in another dead language that gave the secret of Sheba's treasure."

"What is all this leading to?" asked Sir James coldly.

"This, the dearest wish of your life has been to dig up the prehistoric city of El Ab, which lies beneath the desert on the disputed boundary between El Wejh and El Birk. There are certain legends about the place which have kept it inviolate for untold thousands of years. You, like others, believe that at El Ab you will turn up the most valuable secrets of early man. It is even said that at this spot, when it was a garden in the long ago, the first stirrings of Man took form. It would be the greatest feat of any archaeologist to uncover that place and learn what lies there. Ah, that touches you, doesn't it."

Harrison was right. All the cool insouciance of the other was gone. His eyes were glittering, and he was sitting erect.

"How do you know all this?" he demanded curtly.

"I know what it is my business to know. In the same way I know that you bargained with Sheik El Bakr before you left Arabia. You offered him the secret of Sheba's treasure in exchange for permission to excavate the ancient site of El Ab, for protection while doing so, and for financial support. El Bakr refused. He believed he could find the treasure without your aid, and he was determined not to have infidel hands laid on El Ab. Is that true?"

"Possibly."

"I followed Prince Faud from Arabia to England. I came as the personal agent of the Emir El Birk. He also lays claim to El Ab, and it is a claim that is stronger than that of El Bakr. But that does not concern me. What does concern me is the treasure of Sheba. I want my share of that. I am going to have my share. I will kill any person who stands between me and it. I will kill you if necessary, but I am willing to make a bargain with you that will satisfy us both."

"And the bargain is?"

"Give me the secret of the hieroglyphics that tell just where the treasure of Sheba is buried. In return I can promise you, on behalf of the Emir El Bakr, that you shall have a free hand in the excavation of El Ab. You shall have armed protection, and you shall have all the money, labourers and supplies you need."

"But—El Bakr?"

"You can handle Prince Faud easily enough. I know that you have told him nothing yet, beyond warning him to be careful. I know, too, that you tried to send a letter to a certain Hugh Duncan asking his help. It reached him, but not in the way you thought. I intercepted that letter, and dealt with it first. Duncan is now in my hands—here in this house. So that avenue is closed to you. Take your choice. Make a deal with me—or take the consequences!"

Suddenly Harrison's tone changed. It became persuasive.

"Why, Sir James, can't you realise that the chance of your life is here? Your chief hope in regaining your health was to become fit enough to return to Arabia in the hope that you would be able in some way to persuade El Bakr to let you dig up El Ab. Here is your chance. El Bakr can't carry on without money. El Birk must win in the end, and he will dominate the whole of that part of Arabia with his share of the Sheba treasure. He has promised that you shall have a free hand at El Ab, and you know as well as I do that El Birk is known as a man of his word. Now, will you deal with me?"

It is said that every man has his price in some form or other. Not a million pounds in pure gold would have bought the honour of Sir James Pinder. But here before him was being dangled a bribe that bombarded his resistance beyond his strength.

El Ab! The dream of his life! Not an archaeologist, living or dead, but would give or have given his soul for such a chance. To crown his life of work with such a triumph as that. It would place him far, far above any other archaeologist in centuries past or centuries to come. Pinder, the man who first revealed the secret of El Ab! Pinder, who first laid eyes on the beginnings of man! His name would be synonymous with the greatest triumph of archology. It was more than he could resist. He looked at Harrison, and then his eyes dropped in shame as he nodded his surrender.

A snort of triumph burst from Harrison.

"It must be at once," he said crisply. "When can you place the secret in my hands? We must get away from here with the least possible delay—not later than to-morrow."

"It is not here. It is in London."

"Where?"

"In the safe at my house."

"In what form?

"In a small book. It contains a copy of the hieroglyphics and a code translation."

"You will give me a key of the house and of the safe. I'll drive through to London to-night. In the meantime, you can see Prince Faud and fix matters with him. Make him any promises necessary, so that he can get into communication with El Bakr. El Bakr's forces must be withdrawn from the region of El Ab."

"I can tell him something that will serve. But—"

He flushed and then paled.

Harrison laughed.

"Who will think of treachery when you uncover El Ab? No one. It is only results that count in this world. And let me warn you not to try to double-cross me. If you do, I shall take both you and Faud out to sea and dump you there. You know I'm not bluffing."

"Nor am I," said Sir James, turning his eyes away. "I shall keep my word."

Something in his tone satisfied Harrison, and he was a very clever judge of men, crooked or straight.

"All right," he said briskly. "I'll send Prince Faud along to you here. Do your stuff, and El Ab is yours."

Below, in the room where Duncan lay, every word of this conversation had been clearly audible through the microphone that had been fitted secretly to Sir James's rooms as well as to others.

Mary Trent was listening intently. As it proceeded, she began to realise that Harrison was achieving his purpose in a far better way than he had thought possible when he left her. He had believed then that it would be necessary to put Sir James and Prince Faud together, and learn the secret by eavesdropping. But the subtle bribe he had held out had done the trick.

She was sitting with her back to the door. Her eyes were on the figure that lay upon the bed. His eyes were closed, and he seemed scarcely to breathe. There did not seem much likelihood that she would need to make use of the gas pistol that lay on the table close to her hand.

She would have been far less tranquil in her mind had she known that Duncan had been recovering his senses before Harrison came to inspect him, and that he had been shamming stupor while trying to figure out how best to deal with the situation in which he found himself.

But it wasn't from Duncan that Mary Trent needed to fear anything just then. It was something that came from without, and was as amazing to Duncan as it was effective with Mary Trent.

Both of the listeners were completely absorbed in listening to the momentous microphone when the handle of the door behind Mary Trent turned cautiously.

Then the door opened, and a head appeared. Something caused Duncan to raise his lashes slightly so that he could peer out from beneath them. Mary Trent was entirely unsuspicious.

The head that Duncan saw belonged to Hussein, whom he had left in his rooms at Benham. How he had found his way here Duncan couldn't guess, but he could deduce that in some way the Arab suspected that he— Duncan—was being held a prisoner in Grunevald's and that the other had succeeded uncannily in locating his exact whereabouts.

He saw the Arab's gaze rest on him for a moment. Duncan lifted his lids higher and a glance passed between them. Then the door, opened wider and Duncan closed his eyes so as not to attract Mary Trent's attention.

But he could picture the panther-like movements of the Arab as he stalked his prey, could see him creeping stealthily across the space that lay between him and the unconscious girl, until a faint gasp caused Duncan to open his eyes again. He saw Hussin standing over Mary Trent, his hands on her mouth cutting off every sound but the first startled gasp. Duncan was off the bed in a single leap. He reached the table and grasped the gas pistol. He saw that Mary Trent's eyes were open, staring. Duncan gave her a shot of the gas. Then, as she collapsed in a limp heap, he lifted her on to the bed where he had lain.

He faced the Arab, who was scrutinising him gravely.

"Can we get out?" Duncan whispered in Arabic.

"If the effendi will come."

Out of the microphone Duncan could hear Harrison's parting words to. Sir James Pinder: "Do your stuff, and El Ab is yours." Then he made a sign to Hussein, and the two, as alike as twins, vanished from the room.

CHAPTER FIFTEEN

DR. HARRISON received a very nasty jar when he opened the door of that room.

Twenty minutes ago, when he had departed, he had left Mary Trent in a chair with a very effective gas pistol to her hand and Duncan on the bed in a deep state of coma. Now Duncan had vanished and Mary Trent was in his place, her condition being precisely that in which he had believed he had left the private inquiry agent.

Harrison wasted little time in trying to revive her. As soon as he had assured himself that she was really in a gassed state he desisted. He knew only too well the efficacy of that gas, and could not understand even now how Duncan had recovered so soon. As a matter of fact, Duncan would still have been unconscious but for a slight error in Mary Trent's aim. The spray had not struck Duncan with full force upon the mouth and nostrils, but rather along the curve of one cheek.

Leaving her where she lay, Harrison turned and dashed from the room. He was not interested now in overhearing what passed between Sir James Pinder and Prince Faud. If Duncan had been conscious, then he must have heard every scrap of the palaver between him and Sir James. In that case Duncan knew as much as he did, which meant that he had learned what lay in Sir James's safe in London.

He was cursing steadily when he burst like a whirlwind into Dr. Grunevald's room. Grunevald, looking harassed and tired, was writing at his desk.

"Have you seen him?"

The doctor looked blank at the question that Harrison flung at him.

"Who?"

"Duncan—got up as an Arab"

"I haven't seen him. What does it mean? Duncan—an Arab?"

Harrison didn't give him a chance to finish. Racing across the room, be threw open the window. Then he lifted his hand to enjoin silence while he listened. Through the night there came a low, rhythmic sound that was just audible. Then against the sky for a few minutes there appeared in the distance a moving patch of light that Harrison knew could only come from the powerful headlights of a large car. He slammed down the window with an oath. Next moment the telephone receiver was in his hand.

The trunk call he gave was the number of a public-house in Wapping—The Silent Woman. It might be after closing time in London, but that did not perturb Harrison.

His confidence was justified. Within five minutes he was through and when he had satisfied himself as to the identity of the person at the other end of the wire, he barked a question.

"Is Jurgens there?"

"He's in his room."

"Tell him to come to the phone—quick."

Harrison smoked and fumed while he waited, though the period was no more than a few minutes before a thick voice reached him.

"Listen, Jurgens, there's a job for you to do on the jump. Is Max there?"

"Yes—just come in."

"Good! You'll need him. This is a quick job, and nothing to be leery of. I want you to go to forty-three Brinsmead Square, just off Cumberland Place. Got that?"

Yes."

"It is empty at the moment. There isn't even a caretaker there. If you reach it from the back you will find it easy to get in by the last window on the left of the ground floor. Got that?"

"Yes."

"This is straight from the owner himself, so you can depend on it."

"If that is so, why must I break in?"

It was a reasonable enough question, but it caused Harrison to hiss savagely over the wire.

"Don't ask questions. Do as I order. As soon as you get inside, go up the stairs to the first floor. At the end of the hall is a library. In the right-hand corner, as you enter, is a safe. Get ready to take down the combination. Ready?"

"Yes. Go ahead."

"Four right—sixty-five."

"Yes. Four right—sixty-five."

"Three left—forty-eight."

"Three left—forty-eight."

"Two right—sixty."

"Two right—sixty."

"One left—twenty-five."

"One left—twenty-five."

"Then turn the handle."

"Okay. I've got that. What next?"

"You'll have to smash open the inner door. I expected to be there with the keys, but something has happened."

"Okay. That will be easy."

"You will see two small drawers. Open the top one. You will find a small black leather book with a rubber band around it. Take that and close the safe. Then get back to The Silent Woman as quick as you can. I'll meet you there. I'm coming on at once, so you won't have to wait long."

"Okay. Is that all?"

"Not quite. You won't have to worry about the police, but if you do have any trouble don't shoot. That book is the most important thing you've ever bandied. No other trouble can start before I get there. Is that all clear?"

"Sure."

"Very well. Go to it."

With that Harrison rang off. He found Dr. Grunevald gazing at him in stupefaction.

"What does all this mean?" he demanded.

"It means that the storm has broken, Grunevald. Duncan walked in here to-night disguised as an Arab. He got a shot of gas in the face. But he has managed to escape somehow. Mary Trent is the only one who can tell us anything about that, and she is dead to the world. He gave her a shot of the same gas from the same pistol before he escaped."

"But this means disaster. The police will be here any moment."

"No they won't. Duncan, for some reason or other is playing a lone hand. I'll beat him yet."

"What must I do? I am sure the police—"

"You have nothing to do but stay here and do your stuff. Keep your eye on Prince Faud and Sir James Pinder. They're together now. Don't let them out under any pretext. Everything hangs on how we get through this night. Do you understand?"

"Yes. But where are you going?"

"You heard me say just now—London. I've got what I wanted out of Sir James. I'll be back by morning. If Duncan or the police turn up here, use your wits. They haven't a single thing to hang on you."

He waited for no more argument. He knew that if Duncan had been conscious enough to make his escape, he must now be racing at top speed for London.

Jurgens, one of the slickest crooks at large, would do his stuff before Duncan got there, but there was plenty of chance of trouble after that.

He grabbed a hat and plunged out of the front door, calling for Fitzy. A man, one of Grunevald's servants, came stumbling out of the gloom.

He began to stammer something unintelligible. Harrison caught him by the shoulder so fiercely that the fellow broke off with a gasp.

"Where's Fitzy?
"He-he-he's there."

The man pointed with a shaking hand. Harrison dived along the lawn and round some shrubbery. He flashed his torch on something that lay on the grass.

It was Fitzy, his pet gunman, lying like one dead. Looking closer, Harrison saw a lump just where the hair began above the left temple. It needed no more than that to show him that Duncan, or some one in his service, had met Fitzy and dealt with him summarily. It must have been quick work to fix Fitzy before he could reach his gun.

Harrison left him where he lay. He raced back to the car he had left in front; but as he approached it a fresh stream of oaths burst from him. He saw that the offside front tyre was flat. Then the words choked in his throat as he found the near side front tyre in similar condition. And words were utterly beyond him when he found the other two the same. It was a matter of moments to discover that some one had plunged a knife into each cover, and had then dragged it along, making a long slit about three inches long. It was out of the question to think of repairing the tires now. The spare wheel had been slashed too.

He broke into a run, and reached the garage where Dr. Grunevald's cars stood. He found one, and it at least had not been tampered with, but he lost precious time in measuring the petrol in the tank, to find there was only a gallon or so, and then in hunting round until he located some tins of spare petrol, for the chauffeurs were at the station with two of the cars.

It was in a towering rage that he finally backed the big, cumbersome saloon out of the garage, cursing the ark of a vehicle, which was rarely used.

Once out of the gates he drove recklessly. Until he reached Ockham the road was only a secondary one; but there he would turn into the main London-Norwich road, and at that hour of the night he expected to meet little traffic other than a few night-travelling lorries.

But he knew that Duncan was ahead of him, and while he had told Grunevald that Duncan would not go to the police because he was playing a lone hand, he knew there was a very real danger that Duncan would do exactly what he had done—telephone London.

If Duncan had overheard what had passed between him and Sir James Pinder, then the detective would know all that was vital to his case. Harrison had scoffed at any danger from Duncan, but that was because he didn't want Grunevald to crack. He had dreaded the man in India— after the trial. He had dreaded him when he met him here. And he he realised that Duncan was in the thing far deeper than he had suspected and that it would be a matter of hours only before something broke.

With Duncan helpless in his hands he had had nothing to worry about. He knew that even though his assistant were free to act, he would not go and stir up the police for fear of endangering his master.

On the other hand, it was clear enough now that the assistant too had moved swiftly. Mary Trent had blundered. Well, that couldn't be helped. No use blaming her. He himself had looked at Duncan as he lay on the bed and had felt sure that he was still deep under the gas. Duncan had fooled them; but even at that he couldn't have got away without outside assistance.

It never occurred to Harrison that the wandering Arab, Hussein, might have been an active factor in the affair. He did not know that it had been Peter who had sprung upon Fitzy from behind the shrubbery and laid him out before he could get his gun, that Peter and Duncan had raced for their own car while Hussein had remained behind to delay pursuit, that it was Hussein who had slit the tyres of his car, and who would have put Grunevald's out of commission too had he known where to find it. Nor did he know where that same Hussein was still crouching concealed in the grounds, waiting for a chance to strike again.

He did know that Duncan must be racing London-wards at top speed, and he was not wrong in figuring that Duncan might pause long enough on the way to put through a call of warning to Scotland Yard. Harrison knew that Duncan could confide in the higher officials there, and get action, whereas he would hesitate to reveal things to the local police, who were hampered by more cumbersome methods.

That is exactly what Duncan did. At Ipswich he pulled in to a telephone box and put a call through to Scotland Yard. At that hour of the night the officer whom he would have preferred to make contact with, Chief-Inspector Pointer, was off duty.

Inspector Frank Lethbridge took the call, and to him Duncan gave a warning.

"Duncan speaking from Ipswich. I'm on my way to town as fast as I can make it. But it is just possible something may happen before I get there. Will you handle that end of it?"

If I can. Is it in connection with Peel?"

"In a way. I'll tell you all about that later. The immediate danger spot is Brinsmead Square."

"That's a long way from Suffolk. What's doing there?"

"Forty-three Brinsmead Square is the residence of Sir James Pinder, the noted archaeologist."

"I've heard of him. What's he up to?"

"He is not in residence there. An attempt will be made to burgle a safe that stands in the library on the first floor. I want you to have the place surrounded, and keep watch until I get there."

"Right, Mr. Duncan, I'll see to it. If any one turns up we'll gather them in and hold them until you arrive."

"Thanks, Lethbridge. This is very important."

"That's good enough when you say it, Mr. Duncan."

With that Duncan hung up and made for the car. Almost before he was in, Peter had the big Rolls on the move, and they went zooming up the London Road at terrific speed.

They had just left Colchester, behind when Peter laughed aloud.

"What is it, Peter?"

"I was just thinking, sir, how damned queer it is. Here we are burning up the by-pass, and Mr. Harrison is probably doing all he can to overtake us. The crook chasing the 'tec."

"The position may be reversed before the night," is over grunted Duncan.

But at Sir James Pinder's house in Brinsmead Square a complication had arisen that neither Duncan nor Harrison could have foreseen. It was, in fact, Jurgens who quite unwittingly exploded the surprise bomb.

CHAPTER SIXTEEN

BEFORE reaching Ipswich Duncan had managed to get rid of most of his Arab disguise.

It was then, too, that Peter gave him brief details of his imprisonment, of his rescue by Hussein, of their reaching the inn at Benham to find no signs of Duncan, and then of Hussein's shrewd deduction from the condition of the plate containing the remains of his meal of rice and chillies.

"He is no fool," was Duncan's comment. "I am beginning to realise why he occupies a position in the service of the Sheik El Bakr somewhat of the nature of Chief of the Secret Service in this country."

"Yes, sir, any one who takes him for a joke is making a big mistake. I didn't know what was up when I saw his black face on the boat at French Creek."

"I shouldn't be surprised if he knows the countryside by now as well as any local inhabitant, and with his night-prowling I imagine he could tell some of them a few startling things about their movements which they think are entirely unknown. At any rate, he considers himself a colleague of ours, Peter, and I must say that to-night he has proved himself a most valuable ally. But I still don't understand how he found me at Grunevald's."

"We were scouting about the place trying to get a line on what had happened. Then some one jumped up just as I was coming round a bush. I let him have the barrel of my revolver and left him where he fell. Then I took the front, while Hussein took the back. The next I knew the pair of you were coming out on the run. Hussein must have found a way in at the back. And I'll bet he makes a nice job of those tyres before he finishes."

Duncan was silent, leaving it to Peter to guide the big car through the night. He was sorting out in his mind the various pieces of the puzzle that had been accumulating since his journey into Suffolk had plunged him into an entirely unexpected turmoil of developments.

The mild wonder of Scotland Yard over the silence of Detective-Sergeant Peel had become definite uneasiness in Duncan's mind after the finding of Peel's note-book and the deciphering of the code entries, which had seemed to contain references to matters quite outside the range of anything connected with the young Arab noble on whom Peel was supposed to be keeping an eye. The natural conclusion had been that in the course of the one duty Peel had stumbled upon something else which had first roused his definite interest, and later cost him his life.

Duncan had then formed certain tentative theories. Peter's recent experience at French Creek was proof enough that one suspicion at least was sound, and it also confirmed the connection between Frost and the sinister events which had occurred and were still occurring in the district; but just how deeply the fisherman from Little Soham was involved Duncan was not yet ready to hazard.

Then there had been the experience of Peter and himself beneath the van of the itinerant gipsy. No one could have asked for more proof that Lee was mixed up in some nefarious business and it had also brought in an entirely new factor in the form of Dr. Harrison. It was what Duncan had overheard while lying beneath that caravan which enabled him to put his finger on a map of the district and say to Inspector Clark:

"There is the chance that the body of a man may be found here. Let us look."

And, lo and behold, a body had been found. It was the remains of the missing Peel. That had been a further sinister link in the chain, but it was not until Duncan himself had just now overheard the talk between Sir James Pinder and Harrison that he understood the major plot about which, the lesser plots and crimes had revolved.

He was sufficiently learned in archological matters of the Near and Middle East to know of the stone remains which legend said had been erected by the Queen of Sheba on her return journey from the famous visit to King Solomon. Duncan had heard the tale but, like most students, he had looked on it as one of the many romantic legends attaching to the glamorous queen.

It seemed, however, that there was truth in it. Sir James Pinder knew it. The Sheik El Bakr knew it. The Sheik El Birk knew it.

Duncan could now understand the reason for the strength of the enmity that existed between these two emirs. The two princely Arab houses had been warring for generations over that desolate spot, El Ab. Now one could see that it had not been as senseless a warfare as had appeared. The one who held El Ab, and then learned the secret of Sheba's treasure, would own Arabia.

Dr. Raas was but an unimportant unit who had got in some one's way and been swept aside. Harrison would soon dispose of him if he became a danger.

Had Peel blundered upon something linked with the treasure which he was not supposed to know, or had he witnessed the murder of Raas?

And Grunevald? Where did he come in? How deeply involved was he? Had he, like Sir James Pinder, sold himself for some colossal bribe by Harrison? How had Harrison stepped into Grunevald's sanatorium and so quickly assumed direction? Was Grunevald, despite his high reputation, no more than a desperate criminal who up to now had gone undiscovered? Or was he one of Harrison's pawns?

There was no doubt that the black note-book which lay in Sir James Pinder's safe was the keynote of the whole affair. That was the major object of Harrison's plotting. Never mind how he had first learned about the secret; there is an enormous lot of strange whisperings in the bazaars of the East. It was enough that he did know, and once in possession of the book, he would lose no time in vanishing from England. If he succeeded in making contact with the Sheik El Birk with that book there would be big trouble in Arabia.

The fact that it was in connection with these things that Peel had lost his life made it imperative that once he was in London Duncan should lay all his cards before the officials at Scotland Yard. It was also probable that the Commissioner would consider it advisable to communicate with the Foreign Office.

Sheik El Bakr was a friend of this country. Sheik El Birk was a slippery customer who, it was suspected, received finances from sources which were inimical to British influence. The Yard might desire that the F.O. should get in touch first with the Suffolk County Constabulary before they made any approach. In that case, it would mean they would still depend upon Duncan to take care of their interests.

At Liverpool Street Peter stopped the car again while Duncan telephoned once more to the Yard. If there were no definite news there by now, he would continue straight on to Brinsmead Square. If there were news be would proceed to the Yard.

He got Inspector Lethbridge almost at once, and found that officer puzzled.

"As we arrived at Sir James Pinder's house," he said, "we saw a man come out of the gate and get into a waiting taxi. I hailed the taxi but it shot away. We entered the house, and everything seemed all right. No one had touched the safe."

Duncan listened in silence, his face very grave.

"I don't like it, Lethbridge," he said. "The man you saw seems to me very suspicious. Harrison is behind this, and he has many clever agents. Anyway, we had better race along to Brinsmead Square."

Half an hour later the door of the safe in Sir James Pinder's library swung open for the second time that night. There was no outward sign to show that it had been tampered with, but the inner door revealed tell-tale marks where Jurgens had taken no trouble to conceal his forcing of the lock.

Had Duncan needed any more to tell him that his suspicions were only too well founded, he had it when the small drawers were opened.

There was no sign of the black book.

CHAPTER SEVENTEEN

NEEDLESS to say, Dr. Harrison was highly elated over his successful coup.

He reached London some time after Duncan, but, as he intended proceeding no farther than Wapping, he managed to steer Grunevald's heavy saloon down the street at the side of a questionable public-house, The Silent Woman, just about the time that Duncan was drawing a blank at Brinsmead Square.

His arrival was apparently expected, for as he swung in towards the closed doors of the old stable behind the pub, they opened automatically to permit the car to drive straight through.

The doors closed behind him, a light came on, and Harrison saw Tom Jurgens standing inside.

"Well, did you get it?"

"Of course I got it."

Jurgens took the vital book from his pocket and handed it up to Harrison. One quick look was enough to show Harrison that Sir James had not been double-crossing him. It was what he wanted; but Jurgens's sour voice claimed his ear.

"What's that?" Harrison demanded, looking up.

"What was the idea of the bulls? Were you trying to plant us in a trap?"

"What the devil are you talking about?"

"What I say—the flatties. They turned up just as I was leaving, but I managed to get away safely."

For a moment Harrison was puzzled. Then he knew the truth. Duncan had not been slow in putting the police machinery into motion, but he had been too late. Harrison grinned as he dug into a pocket and took out a packet of notes.

"That was an accident," he reassured Jurgens. "You got away, that's the main thing."

"They hailed us. But my pal, who was driving, put his foot on it."

"They didn't follow?"

"No, but they must have got the number of the taxi, and they'll be combing the town for the cab."

"Let them. They won't find it. Here's five hundred. Split it between you as you wish."

Jurgens took the money and stuffed it into his pocket. Quick results were what Harrison wanted, and he got them; quick money was what Jurgens wanted, and he got that. Everything was satisfactory as far as he was concerned. If the police could trail that taxi now they were welcome to do so, and even if they did find it they couldn't connect him with the job.

His self-satisfaction might have received a slight jar had he been aware that, all unknown to Harrison, there had been a passenger curled up inside the luggage guard on the top of the big saloon ever since it had left the grounds of Grunevald's sanatorium.

Hussein had seized his opportunity as the vehicle lumbered past him, and the problem of swinging aboard was easy to one who could reach the saddle of an Arab pony when it was in full gallop.

It had added considerably to the misery which Hussein was already undergoing in this strange land. It was not as rough a ride as he would have endured on a camel, but it was, to him, a plunge into the unknown. He hadn't the remotest idea whither the car was bound. He only knew he had overlooked it when his job had been to attend to any vehicle by which a quick get-away could be effected, and he was still imbued with the idea that, as an accepted colleague of the distinguished British detective, he must hold up his own end.

Therefore through the English night this unhappy Arab had gone speeding London-wards, not suspecting until he was within the outer limits of the metropolis that he was among the bazaars of the great Mecca of the West.

By day, or even at any other than the "dead" hour of the night, he would have been spotted and challenged somewhere along the journey, but not for a single moment did Harrison suspect that he was carrying a passenger, though Hussein came very close to discovery when the big car swung into the narrow streets of the districts surrounding The Silent Woman.

The Arab was over the end and down to the ground just in time to escape being carried into the stable garage. Even then, had it not been that the spot was out of direct line with the rear window of the pub, where a cautious eye was on watch, he would have been seen. But by the time the doors had closed after Harrison, Hussein was already fading like a shadow along the opposite wall.

Duncan was still in conference with Inspector Lethbridge when an orderly entered to present a slip of paper to his superior. Lethbridge frowned over it for a moment, and then looked up.

"What does it mean? Who brought it?"

"An odd fellow was picked up in Commercial Road, sir. He seemed to be in trouble of some sort, and was taken along to the police station. As soon as he got there he asked for paper and pencil, and wrote that down. The sergeant in charge thought the best thing to do was to send him along here."

"You've got him?"

"Yes, sir."

"Wait a moment."

Lethbridge handed the slip of paper to Duncan.

On it, written in painful script, were the two words, "Scotland Yard," and then beneath in Arabic characters, "I am Hussein ben Mustapha, of the personal service of the Sheik El Bakr of El Wejh."

"Can you read that, Mr. Duncan?"

"Quite easily." He translated. "I can only make a guess as to how this individual has managed to get to

London so quickly, but if this was written by the person I know by the same name, then all I can say is he's a marvel!"

"Do you mean to say you know him?"

"I not only know him but am greatly indebted to him for a service he did me earlier this same night down in Suffolk."

"But what's he doing up here? And what does he want of Scotland Yard?"

"He may be trying to find me. I suggest you have him up."

Lethbridge gave instructions to the constable, and a few minutes later the door opened to admit the Arab. For a moment, at sight of Duncan, his Arab reserve cracked in an eager gesture, but then he was quickly grave again as he salaamed to the pair. Lethbridge left it to Duncan to do the talking.

"You have travelled quickly," Duncan began. "I believed you were still at a great distance from here."

"Effendi, may Allah pardon me, but the work thou didst leave me to do is unfinished. I knew not that there was another of the wagons to be attended to. It was only when it came within my sight that Allah opened my eyes. Then it was too late. I had but a moment to make a decision. My poor wits were as the brain of a sulky camel and would not move. So, effendi, I gave myself into the care of Allah and travelled with it. I knew that I had reached some part of this great city, for the bazaars were all about me. But I did not know how I should reach the effendi in such confusion, and the effendi knows that my tongue is useless. So Allah gave me wit again. I had found the effendi once through the servants of the vizier who rules this great palace; therefore, Allah told me to try again."

"You arrived unknown to the one who drove the car?"

"Even so, effendi. I mounted to the top even as one would cling to a Nejd camel."

"How did you descend?"

"I reached the ground, effendi, just before the car passed into an abode."

"It was in the part of the city where you found the police?"

"I had walked some time, effendi."

"You could find it again?"

"It is easier than the deeper bazaars of my country, effendi."

"And this one who drove the car—did you know him?"

"Effendi, it was the same whom I have seen at other times. He came from the palace in great haste and anger."

Duncan turned to the puzzled inspector.

"What he is trying to tell me in a very modest way, Lethbridge, is that he has done a fine piece of work tonight, which is all the more remarkable in that he is in an entirely strange country. As far as I can gather, he has travelled up from Suffolk on the top of a car driven by one who is, I believe, none other than Dr. Harrison. It seems that Harrison vanished into some place in the East End. Mr. Hussein here believes he can take us to it. If he is right, then it is some place where he expects to collect what was taken from Sir James Pinder's safe. I think this is a case for quick action."

Duncan rose. "I'm going after Harrison. Are you coming?"

"I told you my instructions were to work with you."

"Come on, then."

Peter led the way to the big Rolls, Lethbridge and Duncan following. Behind them came a police car packed with plain-clothes men. They would pick up a cruising flying-squad car on the way through the city. They met it at Ludgate Circus. Then the procession raced up Ludgate Hill and into Cannon Street at top speed.

It was to the Leman Street Police Station in the H Division that the wandering Arab had been taken, so this was their destination to see if the constable who had picked him up could give them any directions.

He was only able, however, to give them a general idea of how the man had appeared, so then, driving along to a point which Hussein recognised, they were forced to proceed slowly while he picked out the way.

Dawn was just breaking. A couple of scavenging cats slunk into an alley. A milk roundsman stopped to gaze at the display of police force. A shabby man vanished with the speed of a frightened rat as the police finally tumbled out to form a cordon round The Silent Woman, while Duncan, Lethbridge and Peter dived for the door that opened into an alley at the rear.

It opened at a turn of the handle. If they had expected to meet with opposition they were disappointed. Inside in the hall a single night-light burned. Everything was perfectly quiet and orderly.

They mounted the stairs to encounter a yawning man in pyjamas and dressing-gown. He started back in startled surprise, real or assumed, at sight of the intruders. Then Lethbridge had him by the shoulder.

"Well, Charlie, you're a pretty good bluffer, aren't you? I suppose the whole place could be overrun with people and you wouldn't know a blessed thing about it— just come out yawning like the innocent babe you are, eh?"

But they got nothing out of the man, and nothing came of the search. Nor was there any sign of Harrison.

Duncan went out of the place on the run. He was dead tired; for two nights now he and Peter had had little or no sleep, and both had been through a gruelling time, but every faculty told him that Harrison was already on his way down to Suffolk, and the same reasoning told him that unless he caught him before he reached French Creek, he would never recover the book on which everything hung.

He flung a word to Lethbridge, then tumbled into the car, with Hussein sticking as close as a brother. Peter needed no urging. He turned the car eastwards and pressed the accelerator level with the floorboards.

CHAPTER EIGHTEEN

HARRISON had the better part of an hour's start, but he was handicapped by the cumbersome car.

Nevertheless, he gave it all it would take, and there was no need to worry about pertol or oil. Jurgens had seen to both before he left on his return journey, and before he made his own getaway. But that hour was not too much advantage with Duncan's fast machine burning the road behind him, and Harrison knew it. He did not fool himself that he had got away without leaving a hot chase to follow. What Jurgens had told him about the police trap at Brinsmead Square was enough to warn him that Duncan was moving fast. But Harrison told himself that he could move just one jump faster.

Duncan did not know how close Lethbridge might be following. At no time during the mad race through the early hours of the dawn did he catch the slightest glimpse of the police car. Nor did he waste time by telephoning ahead to the police of Colchester or Ipswich. His sole objective was to overtake Harrison and retrieve the black book before it was gone beyond hope. No police would avail in that while Harrison was on his present course.

But it was evident that the telephone had been put in use, by Lethbridge, for as they thundered into Colchester a constable stood in the middle of the road waving his arms.

The brakes screamed as Peter brought the big car to a stop. The constable stepped to the side. "Mr. Duncan?"

"Yes, what is it?"

"Inspector Lethbridge of Scotland Yard has telephoned through. He says he is following, and wants you to give the exact directions so that I can tell him when he gets here."

Duncan rapped out the necessary details. Then: "Seen another car?"

"A big saloon went through about twenty minutes ago, sir."

"Twenty minutes. All right. On, Peter!"

They flashed through Ipswich. No one intercepted them there. Then they were in the winding country road that would bring them to Ockham.

Approaching Grunevald's estate, Peter proceeded more cautiously. Whether Harrison had arrived or not, Duncan knew that a showdown must come soon.

He had tried to figure out what course Harrison would follow now that he had in his possession the book that held the secret which he had waded through a welter of crime to secure. Nothing now would hold him in England. With the key to the treasure of Sheba in his possession, his next move was Arabia. It was reasonable to suppose that he would make every effort to slip out of England as quickly as possible; but there were his accomplices. He could not leave them to tell all they knew. Duncan believed that Harrison would make first for the sanatorium.

Would Grunevald decamp with Harrison? Or was his share, one that could be settled directly and quickly?

And Sir James Pinder. Just where did he stand? Had he yielded to Harrison because he had genuinely succumbed to the bribe offered, or had he been playing for time? Duncan had not been able to see his face while he and Harrison talked, otherwise he might have been able to make a guess.

Then Prince Faud. What would be done about him? It seemed to Duncan that no matter how fast he moved Harrison would be delayed by the necessity to pick up these loose ends; and if, as he supposed further, Harrison had let The Silent Woman for the sanatorium then they had just a chance of reaching him there.

The sun was already up when Harrison drove in through the gates of the sanatorium. The great house stood as quiet and serene as ever. It did not look as though drama had been played within those old walls only a few hours before, nor as if tragedy were still stalking along its ancient corridors.

None of the patients were visible yet. Either Fitzy had recovered or some one had carried him away, for he no longer lay on the grass.

Harrison swung the car in to the front steps and jumped out. He opened the door and stepped into the hail. Not a soul was in sight. But the moment he opened the door of Grunevald's office he found life enough.

Grunevald, unkempt, and clad only in pyjamas and dressing-gown, was pacing the floor in agitation. As Harrison entered he swung round, and a stream of reproaches poured from him.

"What does it mean?" he cried hoarsely. "I have been waiting all these hours for you to come. I never dreamed that things would come to this. You told me there would never be any risk of the police, and now see what happened here in the night! I did not know what was going on. You have fooled me and involved me in very serious things."

"Shut up!"

The words burst from Harrison like a pistol-shot.

"Stop shouting like a fishwife!" he went on raspingly. "We have urgent matters to attend to." Grunevald glowered at him.

"What do you mean?"

"I mean that I have at last secured what I wanted. It is here"—and he touched his coat. "The next thing is to get away. I've got to go on the jump."

"And me—what about me? Am I to stay and be arrested? Am I—Dr. Otto Grunevald—to suffer such indignity?"

"If the police knew how Dr. Otto Grunevald had been engaged for years in smuggling drugs into this country he would have been arrested long ago, my friend. You're a humbug, Grunevald; and now, because you are afraid, you're squealing."

"But the police! Ever since you have come to blackmail me with your knowledge of what I was doing, things have gone wrong. The smuggling of drugs was a medical matter. But—murder . . ."

"Shut up, I tell you!"

Harrison sprang forward, and his face held an expression that caused Grunevald to flinch back.

"You came into this thing with your eyes open. You fell for my plans because you were greedy for money. It was I who did everything. You simply waited for the profits. Well, we've won out. But if you show any signs of betraying me, I'll deal with you as I dealt with others."

"But that man Duncan! I have heard how he was here and escaped. He will not give up. He will expose me, and that means ruin. Something must be done."

Harrison studied the other shrewdly. He could see that Grunevald was on the verge of becoming as acute a nervous wreck as any of his patients. The man was jittering with terror. It would be impossible to trust him now. Besides, what was the need? He had the secret he wanted. Grunevald had served his purpose. There was nothing more to be gained from him. He didn't need him, and he didn't need the sanatorium as a base of operations any longer. Better dispose of this danger now.

"You leave matters to me," he said soothingly, while one hand slipped into his pocket, "I have already settled with Duncan. He won't come here again; nor will the police."

"You—you have killed him too?" gasped Grunevald.

But Harrison only smiled. He had drawn nearer to the other now. If he stretched out his arm he could touch him.

He did stretch out his arm, but he didn't touch Grunevald. Instead, he pressed the trigger of the gas-gun he held, and Grunevald dropped in his tracks.

Harrison returned the gas-gun to his pocket and, catching hold of the unconscious man, dragged him behind the big screen and dumped him on the couch there. Then he proceeded to find Fitzy, the gunman.

He found him, still somewhat groggy, but only too ready to listen to Harrison's instructions.

"Get that typewriter of yours, Fitzy," Harrison told him, "and watch the gates. Some one may turn up at any moment. They are the same people who laid you out last night. When they do come, get yours in first this time or there won't be a second chance for you. Then you and I will clear out."

"I'll give them the works all right," the gunman assured him.

Leaving the man to carry on, Harrison went to find Mary Trent, for he loved this woman—as much as he could love any one. She was still lying on the bed but she was conscious. He told her jubilantly what he had done.

"And now we've got to get away, my dear. Fitzy is outside. He'll take care of any one who shows up. How soon can you be ready?"

"Give me five minutes."

"No more. I'm going along to Sir James and Prince Faud."

"What are you going to do? Don't run more risks."

"My dear girl, leave this to me. Do you think I am such a fool as to leave Sir James to double cross me? It's no time now for half-measures."

He vanished, and Mary Trent rose wearily. When she had first started out as partner to the clever adventurer, Dr. Harrison, it had been with no thought of becoming a killer's woman.

In the beginning it had been no more than robbery, fraud, swindling—any and every slick means of separating some one from his or, her money. But just as the snowball grows as it rolls downhill, so had their criminal deeds grown to greater and greater volume.

Still, she would follow him. Wherever he must go she would go too. Women are like that.

So, while Harrison hastened on his way to carry out the sinister purpose he had formed regarding Sir James Pinder, Mary Trent began to get ready to make still another getaway. But her movements and Harrison's course were arrested by the staccato rattle of Fitzy's sub-machine-gun somewhere out in the grounds.

CHAPTER NINETEEN

PETER drove straight into Fitzy's ambush.

Duncan had been watchful from the moment they approached the estate. He had expected trouble, but that did not deter either him or Peter; and Hussein seemed to take it all as a matter of course.

Fitzy had chosen his spot well. He was planted with the sub-machine-gun in the midst of a dump of shrubbery that commanded the drive from the gate almost to the house. Nothing could pass in or out and escape the spitting range of the vicious weapon which he held at hip level.

Harrison had told him to give the works to anything that came in. He obeyed.

Peter bent low over the wheel. He was counting on the bullet-proof qualities of the car. It wouldn't be the first time that Fitzy had turned a deadly fusillade upon it.

Duncan, however, did not remain passive under the attack. He knew instinctively why the ambush had been placed. And he figured, too, that the man behind the sub-machine-gun would be one of Harrison's chief assets.

So, with the bullets spattering the car like hail, he jerked his automatic upon the shrubbery from which the fusillade was coming.

Bullets whistled past his ears and crashed against the proof-glass behind him. One slug struck the frame of the window close to his head and took his hat clean off. But Duncan emptied his revolver into the heart of the ambush, and suddenly the hail of lead stopped. It might have been because he had scored a hit, or it might be that the drum was momentarily empty. He did not pause to find out. Instead, he drew back and quickly stuffed a fresh clip into his own weapon, while Peter finished the short distance at a truly terrific speed.

It was now that Duncan would have been glad to have had Lethbridge and his men along. He knew that they were thundering down the road as fast as possible, but this was the critical moment.

He and Peter tumbled out. He sent Peter to the rear to stop the bolt-holes there while he attacked the front door. It was impossible to open it from the outside without a key, and the ambush they had already encountered told him that they were expected.

He sent a couple of bullets into the lock. It is by no means as easy to shoot open a lock as is generally assumed, but on this occasion the luck was with Duncan. He grabbed the handle and turned it. The door gave. He stepped into the hall and saw no one. The absence of resistance made him all the more wary. He did not know that Harrison was already coming down on the run from an upper floor.

Duncan made first for Grunevald's office. The door opened readily enough. He stepped into what he thought was an empty room, his gun ready.

Behind the screen he saw the unconscious Grunevald where Harrison had dumped him. Whatever might happen later, he was no longer a factor to be counted.

Duncan turned back and made for the hall. He heard a shot somewhere in the distance and thought Peter must be in action.

Out in the hall again, he heard a noise above him. He looked up and saw Harrison just before the other began to shoot.

Duncan swung to one side, so that the stairs gave him some cover. Then he moved towards the front of the hall until the slope of the stairs was too low for him to stand upright. Harrison had stopped shooting. Duncan knew he was waiting. There was no need for words. Each knew that the thing had come to a showdown, and why.

Then Duncan made a rush as Harrison began shooting again.

In four places lead ripped through Duncan's clothing, and two bullets seared his flesh, but no serious hit was made as he rushed in zigzags towards the man firing.

Suddenly Harrison vanished. One moment he was there, the next he was gone. Duncan thought he must have dived into some room near at hand, and covered the last few steps at a bound.

Then he saw Harrison some distance along the landing. He saw some one else too. It was Mary Trent. They were running towards a bend farther down, and vanished round this.

Duncan plunged after them. He was about halfway down the passage when a door opened and some one lurched in his path. To his amazement it was Frost. He was reeling along as if badly wounded, and on his heels came Peter his revolver still smoking.

Duncan grasped the situation in a flash. Peter must have flushed Frost in the kitchen quarters and had to fight him up the back stairs. Indeed, now he could see that they had emerged from a landing at the head of a flight. Then he was past the opening, and turning his revolver to meet Frost's threat as he backed against the wall.

But that effort was all that Frost could summon. While he struggled to get his gun up, he collapsed in a heap and rolled over. Peter's bullets had got him somewhere.

Together now Duncan and Peter rushed into the branching passage. They could see no signs of Harrison and Mary Trent, but they could hear them clattering down another flight of stairs at the end of the passage. They dived after them, catching a fleeting glimpse of the pair as they vanished at the bottom.

They tumbled down the stairs and burst into a large kitchen. Several servants were gathered there in a state of terror. There had been loud screams as Dr. Harrison, a revolver in his hand, had charged through them, Mary Trent with him. And now came further screams as Duncan and Peter, looking even more dangerous, rushed after the fugitives.

Duncan could only think that Dr. Harrison must be trying to reach the car he had left in front, though he knew it was quite on the cards that Harrison would take his own car if he came to it first.

Neither he nor Peter knew what had become of Hussein. He had been lost in the first hasty scuffle. Nor was Duncan anxious for him to become involved in anything as strenuous as this. He didn't want to put the Foreign Office in a situation where it would have too much to explain.

Hussein, however, was by no means inactive, as they saw when they passed from the kitchen through a corridor that led to a back door. Through this Harrison and Mary Trent had already vanished. Duncan and Peter reached it just in time to see an extraordinary thing.

They did not know that Frost had arrived on his motor-cycle to find out why Harrison had not turned up that night as arranged. He had come, just in time to find himself involved in something that he would have given much to escape. Now Harrison was making use of Frost's motor-cycle to further his own escape.

When Duncan and Peter burst into the open, Harrison was already turning the machine towards the drive that ran round from the front. Mary Trent was running behind him, ready to get astride the pillion, and across the grass they saw Hussein leaping like a Barbary sheep, the tail of his turban flying, a wicked-looking knife raised aloft.

He changed his course so as to intercept the motorcycle. Harrison did not take time to shoot; he evidently counted on being able to steer the machine round the danger. He had forgotten the ability of the average Arab to swing aboard a galloping horse.

As Harrison got the motor-cycle going, and as Mary Trent leapt on to the pillion while it was in motion, Hussein launched himself full at the oncoming danger.

To Harrison it was an entirely unexpected move. The result was disastrous for the moment. As the Arab's long sinewy hand grasped him, the motorcycle careened to one side, and then the whole outfit brought the three of them crashing to the ground.

Hussein rolled clear, and in a trice was upon Harrison. Still running, Duncan and Peter saw the knife flash twice, but they could not discern exactly what was going on, so inextricably were the three mixed up with the machine.

Suddenly they saw Harrison spring clear. There was something odd in his appearance which they could not understand at first. Then they saw that only a shred of his coat was left on him. Hussein seemed to have slashed it clean away in those two strokes of the knife.

Harrison righted the machine and gave a hand to Mary Trent, who was standing as if dazed. He swung her over the pillion and started again. Hussien lay on the ground—motionless.

Duncan and Peter fired, but desisted when Mary Trent came between them and their target. Harrison had the motor-cycle going well now, and as it gathered speed went careering round the corner of the house out of sight.

Duncan and Peter could do no more than stop to see if Hussein was badly hurt, but the Arab was now getting to his feet. He had only been stunned. With one hand he held the remnants of Harrison's coat, with the other he was fumbling among the rags.

Then he produced something which caused Duncan to utter an exclamation of deep satisfaction. It was the black book that had been taken from the sate in Brinsmead Square.

"The effendi will do me the honour to receive this. It is the will of Allah that I am the means of restoring it."

Duncan grabbed it. He thrust it deep into an inner pocket as he ran on again. He believed he knew by what way Harrison would try to escape, and he thought he might still stop him.

For escape was all that remained to Harrison now. Hussein had cut from him with that knife, in two swift strokes, all that he had gained in a series of terrible crimes.

Duncan and Peter, with Hussein behind them, raced round the house to the front, where Duncan's car stood. They could hear the racketeering of the motor-cycle as Harrison tore down the drive.

They tumbled into the car, and Peter took the wheel. Hussein followed. He was evidently determined to be in at the death. Peter gave Duncan a glance that asked a question.

"Not French Creek. Make for Little Soham. We'll try and cut them off as they come out of French Creek into the river."

The car leaped ahead. It gathered speed as they went down the drive until just before they reached the gates the speedometer was already showing close to fifty. Then, just as Peter was about to swing into the road, he was obliged to jam his brakes with such force that the big car screamed in protest.

The police car, with Lethbridge aboard, was just turning in. A head-on collision was avoided by less than an inch. Precious moments were lost while the way was cleared. Duncan made hurried explanations to Lethbridge, then both cars took the road for Little Soham.

Their arrival in the village created the biggest sensation that had been known there for many a year, but Duncan's eyes were not for the curious. He was staring ahead, watching for just one little thing—Frost's speed-boat, the one he had seen on his first visit to Little Soham.

Several fishermen on the small jetty gaped as they tumbled out. He knew that if there was no further delay it would be touch and go whether they reached the mouth of the French Creek before Harrison appeared in the other craft.

Luck was with them in that the boat was afloat. Duncan did not know about the petrol and the oil. He had to take a chance on that.

Lethbridge had only a hazy idea of what Duncan was about. In the wild dash from the sanatorium to Little Soham, Duncan had only found it possible to jerk out a few details.

Lethbridge realised that he had missed a vital moment in some way. Yet he was not altogether to blame. Ordinary police duty had made it impossible for him to leave The Silent Woman as soon as Duncan and Peter.

He did not know the real depth of desperate plot and counter-plot behind Duncan's actions. Scotland Yard had not yet learned how and why Detective-Sergeant Peel had died. But he was ready enough to follow Duncan, even though there must be an explanation later to the Suffolk County Police as to why he was in that county without the official cognizance of the Chief Constable. The plainclothes men were prepared to follow Lethbridge to the limit. He was what is known among those of the lesser grade as one of the best."

Thus it was with this motley company that Abel Frost's speed-boat, usually employed in the mildly interesting job of conveying tourists up and down the river between Little Soham and the sea, turned her nose down-stream on a far more desperate venture than her builder had ever contemplated.

Peter was in the cockpit. The engine was, naturally, his job. Duncan had taken the steering-wheel. He brought the boat round in a water-skid that caused the assembled fishermen on the jetty to gape. They had never before seen a boat turned in that fashion, and their astonishment was all the greater because they recognised in Duncan the same man who had appeared in Little Soham before.

They were wondering, too, why this stranger was making free with Frost's boat, but they made no move to interfere. Frost was a queer bird: they had learned to leave him alone.

They were still gaping when the speed-boat came into the straight and went down-stream at ever-gathering speed.

Duncan didn't know the channel of the river, but he wasn't worrying about that. There were certain usual indications in the form of the scouring of the banks which gave him a more or less general idea of how the channel had been cut by the force of the current, but that was all. If they struck the mud then all was finished.

He held the wheel loosely, almost negligently, for across the marshes his eyes were seeking the French Creek. Then he caught one fleeting glimpse of what he sought. Above a break in the low bank of the creek he saw something flash past. He knew it could only be the camouflaged speed-boat. Harrison had reached his objective. He was all out in a last desperate bid for liberty.

Duncan shouted to Peter to give the engine all it had. He made signs that told the lad he had seen the other boat, and that Peter could govern himself accordingly.

On they swept. One of the London policemen put his head over the side. This was not the sort of thing he was accustomed to. The others hung on grimly. Then all of a sudden the opening of French Creek came into view. A little distance farther on, rushing towards it at an even greater speed than they were approaching, was another boat. Duncan could see Harrison crouching in the cockpit. Mary Trent was not visible.

He signed again to Peter, then he started back towards Lethbridge and crouched beside him, watching the other craft, trying to calculate which would reach the junction first.

As he figured it, they should just do it first. In that case there was only one thing to do, to slow down at the vital moment and place their boat right across the narrow entrance. Harrison would have to do one thing or the other—slow down, stop and reverse, or else come straight on. If the latter, then some quick handling would be necessary.

Duncan stood up. Harrison could see him now, but gave no sign. Nearer and nearer the two rushing boats drew. It looked to Duncan and to those with him as though the boat were going too fast; and Harrison showed not the slightest sign of slowing down.

Then things began to happen so fast that it was impossible to keep track of them. Peter was already throttling down desperately, but it was too late. Straight across the mouth of French Creek went their boat, and straight upon it came the far larger and heavier boat in which Harrison was travelling.

There could be only one result. The larger boat cut through the smaller like a knife through butter. There was a terrific upheaval, a great surging of water, and then a violent explosion as the smaller craft burst into flame.

Harrison managed somehow to keep his boat in direction. He swung it round, and then was gone downstream while Duncan and his companions struggled in the water.

Needless to say, both the Foreign Office and Scotland Yard were deeply gratified with Duncan's handling of what had turned out to be a very serious plot against a friendly foreign potentate, and were further indebted to him for his discovery of the large drug and liquor traffic which there was no doubt had been operating merrily through Little Soham for a considerable time past.

Dr. Grunevald was, of course, ruined by the exposures. He was sentenced to a long term of imprisonment, after which he would be deported. Yet, though he undoubtedly deserved his fate, Duncan could not but regret such an ending to the career of a man of his gifts. No matter what his faults, his research work was of immense value to humanity. Aside from the criminal practices into which his overweening enthusiasm and need of money had led him, the sanatorium had been run on a perfectly honest basis, and had it not been for the fact that the master spell-binder, Dr. Harrison, had crossed his path, discovered his weak spots, and exploited them, the good he was doing would probably have outweighed the evil. Duncan held that he wasn't the first man who had been plunged to ruin through Harrison.

The most poignant moment in the whole affair, however, was when Duncan and Sir James Pinder sat alone in the latter's room at the sanatorium.

It was strange indeed that this man, so full of years and high achievement, should be sitting with shamed eyes and bowed head before one so much younger. Yet, had he been able to meet the other's gaze, he would have found it tempered with pity.

"It seems impossible that any one will ever understand, Duncan," he was saying huskily. "It wasn't physical fear. I have never experienced that in my life. Nor am I afraid of dying. I am old and have had a good inning."

"What was it, then, Sir James, that caused you to do it? The Sheik El Bakr was a good friend to you."

"I know, I know. That is what shames me. I would not try to justify myself to another soul on earth, Duncan, but you must understand. Whether you believe it or not, at first I hoped to keep that devil stalled until you could take some action against him. You remember that I did write you a letter?"

"Which Harrison intercepted."

"I didn't know that. I swear it."

"I believe you, Sir James."

"But I will be absolutely honest. It was the terrible temptation that he dangled before me."

"You mean El Ab?"

"Yes—El Ab. No one knows what that name means to me. During all the years I have dug into the past El Ab has been the Golden Fleece that beckoned me. It seemed at times that I would sell my soul to have a free hand there. But even though I appeared to have yielded to temptation, I could not have done it. You must believe that."

"I do, Sir James. And since you mean that, there is only one thing for you to do—so Chief-Inspector Pointer of Scotland Yard has sent me to say."

"What is that?"

"Go out to El Wejh and see the Sheik El Bakr. Tell him everything. Tell him just what sort of deal Harrison had made with his enemy, the Sheik El Birk. We hope to catch Harrison before he gets to Arabia, but he is a slippery customer. Mr. Pointer says it is for you to reach there first and prepare Sheik El Bakr."

"He thinks that would help?"

"He does. And I know it would."

"Then I will go, Duncan—I will go. But what if the truth gets out?"

"I am also to say that it need never be known. You will not talk, nor will we. Mr. Pointer further suggests that you take Prince Faud with you. He knows nothing, need know nothing. Then, when you get there, you can give your personal service to El Bakr and help him find the treasure of Sheba. Personally, I am willing to prophesy that in return for this you will find him inclined to give you your heart's desire."

The other caught his arm.

"You mean?" he gasped.

"El Ab."

And, indeed, Duncan's words were prophetic, for some months later the journal of one of the learned societies held the portentous announcement that the Sheik El Bakr of El Wejh had, as a mark of long friendship, conferred upon the distinguished archaeologist, Sir James Pinder, the coveted sole right to proceed with the excavations on the site of the legendary city of El Ab, believed to be the most ancient site of man's first community.

Duncan may be excused a brief smile when he read the announcement.

If these things had their sombre side, there was another feature that stood out in marked contrast. This was the official reception of one Hussein at Scotland Yard by the Commissioner and a high personage from the Foreign Office.

Hussein arrived in Duncan's car garbed in all the picturesque raiment of a high official of the Court of the Sheik El Bakr of El Wejh, and his reception was of such a gratifying nature that on his return to Arabia it took many evenings, and many, many cups of black coffee, to cover the period of the picturesque tale he had to tell to his master El Bakr.

But what pleased him most of all was the fact that these high officials of Scotland Yard received him, not so much as a court representative of El Wejh, but as the Chief of the Secret Service of that country. Secretly he had always held Scotland Yard and the British Secret Service in the deepest awe and respect. And now to be accepted as a colleague! To be referred to and made a fuss of as having accomplished great things in this Western land! By Allah, but there was something here to put into the ear of the fat grand vizier when he got home. This tale would make him shift his carcase when he babbled about dirty dogs of bazaar thieves.

Nor did his gratifying experience end there. When he finally left England in company with Prince Faud and Sir James Pinder, it was to find himself the centre of a group of uniformed men who gave him a parting salute fit for an emir himself.

The last man whose hand he shook, and the last upon whom he called Allah's blessing, was Duncan. There, he felt, was his true colleague, one who understood all. For had he not, by his magic, summoned up rice and chillies in an outlandish caravanserai where such things had not seemed to exist? By Allah, yes, Duncan effendi was a great man.

THE END

Other Resurrected Press Books in *The Chief Inspector Pointer Mystery* Series

AVAILABLE FROM RESURRECTED PRESS!

THE EDWARDIAN DETECTIVES
LITERARY SLEUTHS OF THE EDWARDIAN ERA

The exploits of the great Victorian Detectives, Poe's C. Auguste Dupin, Gaboriau's Lecoq, and most famously, Arthur Conan Doyle's Sherlock Holmes, are well known. But what of those fictional detectives that came after, those of the Edwardian Age? The period between the death of Queen Victoria and the First World War had been called the Golden Age of the detective short story, but how familiar is the modern reader with the sleuths of this era? And such an extraordinary group they were, including in their numbers an unassuming English priest, a blind man, a master of disguises, a lecturer in medical jurisprudence, a noble woman working for Scotland Yard, and a savant so brilliant he was known as "The Thinking Machine."

To introduce readers to these detectives, Resurrected Press has assembled a collection of stories featuring these and other remarkable sleuths in The Edwardian Detectives.

- The Case of Laker, Absconded by Arthur Morrison
- The Fenchurch Street Mystery by Baroness Orczy
- The Crime of the French Café by Nick Carter
- The Man with Nailed Shoes by R Austin Freeman
- The Blue Cross by G. K. Chesterton
- The Case of the Pocket Diary Found in the Snow by Augusta Groner
- The Ninescore Mystery by Baroness Orczy
- The Riddle of the Ninth Finger by Thomas W. Hanshew
- The Knight's Cross Signal Problem by Ernest Bramah

- The Problem of Cell 13 by Jacques Futrelle
- The Conundrum of the Golf Links by Percy James Brebner
- The Silkworms of Florence by Clifford Ashdown
- The Gateway of the Monster by William Hope Hodgson
- The Affair at the Semiramis Hotel by A. E. W. Mason
- The Affair of the Avalanche Bicycle & Tyre Co., LTD by Arthur Morrison

RESURRECTED PRESS CLASSIC MYSTERY CATALOGUE

Journeys into Mystery
Travel and Mystery in a More Elegant Time

The Edwardian Detectives
Literary Sleuths of the Edwardian Era

Gems of Mystery
Lost Jewels from a More Elegant Age

E. C. Bentley
Trent's Last Case: The Woman in Black

Ernest Bramah
Max Carrados Resurrected:
The Detective Stories of Max Carrados

Agatha Christie
The Secret Adversary
The Mysterious Affair at Styles

Octavus Roy Cohen
Midnight

Freeman Wills Croft
The Ponson Case
The Pit Prop Syndicate

J. S. Fletcher
The Herapath Property
The Rayner-Slade Amalgamation
The Chestermarke Instinct
The Paradise Mystery
Dead Men's Money

The Middle of Things
Ravensdene Court
Scarhaven Keep
The Orange-Yellow Diamond
The Middle Temple Murder
The Tallyrand Maxim
The Borough Treasurer
In the Mayor's Parlour
The Saftey Pin

R. Austin Freeman
*The Mystery of 31 New Inn from the Dr. Thorndyke
Series*
*John Thorndyke's Cases from the Dr. Thorndyke
Series*
The Red Thumb Mark from The Dr. Thorndyke Series
The Eye of Osiris from The Dr. Thorndyke Series
A Silent Witness from the Dr. John Thorndyke Series
The Cat's Eye from the Dr. John Thorndyke Series
*Helen Vardon's Confession: A Dr. John Thorndyke
Story*
As a Thief in the Night: A Dr. John Thorndyke Story
*Mr. Pottermack's Oversight: A Dr. John Thorndyke
Story*
*Dr. Thorndyke Intervenes: A Dr. John Thorndyke
Story*
The Singing Bone: The Adventures of Dr. Thorndyke
The Stoneware Monkey: A Dr. John Thorndyke Story
*The Great Portrait Mystery, and Other Stories: A
Collection of Dr. John Thorndyke and Other Stories*
The Penrose Mystery: A Dr. John Thorndyke Story
The Uttermost Farthing: A Savant's Vendetta

Arthur Griffiths
The Passenger From Calais
The Rome Express

Fergus Hume
The Mystery of a Hansom Cab
The Green Mummy
The Silent House
The Secret Passage

Edgar Jepson
The Loudwater Mystery

A. E. W. Mason
At the Villa Rose

A. A. Milne
The Red House Mystery
Baroness Emma Orczy
The Old Man in the Corner

Edgar Allan Poe
The Detective Stories of Edgar Allan Poe

Arthur J. Rees
The Hampstead Mystery
The Shrieking Pit
The Hand In The Dark
The Moon Rock
The Mystery of the Downs

Mary Roberts Rinehart
Sight Unseen and The Confession

Dorothy L. Sayers
Whose Body?

Sir William Magnay
The Hunt Ball Mystery

Mabel and Paul Thorne
The Sheridan Road Mystery

Louis Tracy
The Strange Case of Mortimer Fenley
The Albert Gate Mystery
The Bartlett Mystery
The Postmaster's Daughter
The House of Peril
The Sandling Case: What Would You Have Done?
Charles Edmonds Walk
The Paternoster Ruby

John R. Watson
The Mystery of the Downs
The Hampstead Mystery

Edgar Wallace
The Daffodil Mystery
The Crimson Circle

Carolyn Wells
Vicky Van
The Man Who Fell Through the Earth
In the Onyx Lobby
Raspberry Jam
The Clue
The Room with the Tassels
The Vanishing of Betty Varian
The Mystery Girl
The White Alley
The Curved Blades
Anybody but Anne
The Bride of a Moment
Faulkner's Folly
The Diamond Pin
The Gold Bag
The Mystery of the Sycamore
The Come Backy

Raoul Whitfield
Death in a Bowl

And much more!
Visit ResurrectedPress.com
for our complete catalogue

About Resurrected Press

A division of Intrepid Ink, LLC, Resurrected Press is dedicated to bringing high quality, vintage books back into publication. See our entire catalogue and find out more at www.ResurrectedPress.com.

About Intrepid Ink, LLC

Intrepid Ink, LLC provides full publishing services to authors of fiction and non-fiction books, eBooks and websites. From editing to formatting, from publishing to marketing, Intrepid Ink gets your creative works into the hands of the people who want to read them. Find out more at www.IntrepidInk.com.

CPSIA information can be obtained at www.ICGtesting.com
Printed in the USA
LVOW10s1457070616

491590LV00014B/711/P